# "I'd like to sweep you off your feet."

David flung his arms out dramatically. "I want to throw you over my shoulder and carry you away with me."

Jennifer laughed. "You've already lured me up to your hotel room." Kicking off her shoes, she draped herself suggestively across his bed and said in her best Lauren Bacall voice, "I'm ready, willing and able to be ravished."

David knelt beside her. In a seductive Cary Grant impersonation he murmured, "I've been fantasizing about this moment since the first time I saw you."

"And I thought you gave me your umbrella in that storm to be chivalrous," she chided.

"That *was* chivalrous. But tonight I'm going to act like a cad."

"David?" Her playful tone was suddenly gone. "Please do...."

**Cassie Miles** says her life is like a comedy. For example, as she neared completion of this, her fourth Temptation, disaster struck. She dropped her purse while she was riding her moped—and it was promptly run over by a convoy of army trucks! The cable for her computer, which she needed to print out *Seems Like Old Times*, was crushed. But Cassie always comes up smiling. We know you'll smile, too, as you read this warm, humorous tale, now safe in our hands.

Cassie lives in Denver, Colorado, with her husband and two daughters. She still rides a moped.

## Books by Cassie Miles

HARLEQUIN TEMPTATION
  26–TONGUE-TIED
  61–ACTS OF MAGIC
 104–IT'S ONLY NATURAL

Don't miss any of our special offers. Write to us at the following address for information on our newest releases.

Harlequin Reader Service
901 Fuhrmann Blvd., P.O. Box 1397, Buffalo, NY 14240
Canadian address: P.O. Box 603,
Fort Erie, Ont. L2A 5X3

# Seems Like Old Times
## CASSIE MILES

### Harlequin Books

TORONTO • NEW YORK • LONDON
AMSTERDAM • PARIS • SYDNEY • HAMBURG
STOCKHOLM • ATHENS • TOKYO • MILAN

Published September 1987

ISBN 0-373-25270-6

Copyright © 1987 by Kay Bergstrom. All rights reserved.
Philippine copyright 1987. Australian copyright 1987.
Except for use in any review, the reproduction or utilization of
this work in whole or in part in any form by any electronic,
mechanical or other means, now known or hereafter invented,
including xerography, photocopying and recording, or in any
information storage or retrieval system, is forbidden without
the permission of the publisher, Harlequin Enterprises Limited,
225 Duncan Mill Road, Don Mills, Ontario, Canada M3B 3K9.

All the characters in this book have no existence outside the
imagination of the author and have no relation whatsoever to
anyone bearing the same name or names. They are not even
distantly inspired by any individual known or unknown to the
author, and all incidents are pure invention.

The Harlequin trademarks, consisting of the words, TEMPTATION,
HARLEQUIN TEMPTATION, HARLEQUIN TEMPTATIONS,
and the portrayal of a Harlequin, are trademarks of Harlequin Enterprises
Limited; the portrayal of a Harlequin is registered in the United
States Patent and Trademark Office and in the Canada Trade
Marks Office.

Printed in Canada

# 1

WITH A SONG in her heart and a smile on her lips Jennifer Watt sauntered across the threadbare, but florid, carpeting in the lobby of the Uptown Theater. Though it was after midnight, she took a moment to glance up at the high vaulted ceiling. The splotchy turquoise trim showed an intricate cobweb of cracks. And the gilt on the cherubs was little more than a nostalgic hint of the former rococo splendor of the aged movie house.

*Beautiful.* To Jennifer it all seemed beautiful, bathed in the rose-tinted glow of the classic movies she'd just viewed at the Classic Cinema Marathon.

Those were the days, she thought. The golden age of motion pictures in the thirties and forties, when the heroines were lovely and the heroes dashing. And the endings were happily happily ever after.

She hummed the title song from *Singin' in the Rain*, the last feature shown, as she exchanged grins with the other die-hard movie fans who straggled toward the exit.

The weather obligingly continued the rainy theme of the movie, but this deluge was nothing to hum about. Rather than a lilting shower, downtown Denver was in the grip of a fierce electric storm.

With a shiver Jennifer folded her arms beneath her breasts. She'd gone straight to the theater from work, and her slim, buttoned-down-the-side skirt and beige linen jacket offered little protection against the elements. Worse yet, her van was parked four blocks away, and she hadn't brought a rain slicker or an umbrella. She hadn't even brought a scarf. It was August, for pity's sake, not a time for chilling thunderstorms.

As she paced back and forth under the marquee, the bounce faded from her step. The movie melodies went quiet in her mind, drowned out by the steady thrum of rain and occasional explosions of thunder.

She huddled beside a colorful poster for *Kiss Me Kate* and muttered to herself, "It has to let up."

"Why?"

The deep-voiced reply startled her. She spun around and gazed up into the most gorgeous smile she'd ever seen—the smile of a matinee idol. Not only did he have perfect teeth, but his smoky gray eyes and thick, sable-colored hair positively gleamed in the neon glare of the marquee. He had dimples like Clark Gable.

It took Jennifer a moment to realize that she was gaping like some idiot heroine of the thirties. With a gulp she closed her mouth and swallowed what was left of her pride. This wasn't the movies. In real life no crescendo of violins heralded the meeting of a man and a woman. There were no softly focused close-ups.

Too bad about the soft-focus, she thought wryly. Standing in the harsh light, she knew that all her rough edges were exposed. Her straight, shoulder-length hair must be drooping, her clothes were wrinkled and her mascara must have smeared when she cried at the poignant ending of *It's a Wonderful Life*.

"Why does it have to let up?" he repeated.

"Because it can't go on raining forever."

Brilliant comeback, she jeered at herself. But who could expect charm in the middle of the night? In a rainstorm? In any case, she shouldn't be striking up midnight conversations with total strangers.

She was old enough to know better. And she certainly had more common sense. Somehow, gazing at this uncommonly handsome man left her as giddy and senseless as a teenager.

Too much cinematic fantasy, she deduced as she purposely looked away from him, noting with relief that they weren't all alone. Several other people had taken shelter under the marquee.

"Were you in the theater?" he asked.

She nodded and edged away from him.

"I hadn't intended to stay for all of *Singin' in the Rain*," he continued. "But I wanted to see Gene Kelly do that splashing-in-the-rain, swinging-on-the-lamppost dance. The title number. It's a great movie moment. After that I was hooked."

Jennifer recognized the enthusiasm of a true classic cinema buff in the way he eyed the puddles from the torrential downpour. Was he actually considering a reprise?

"A great movie moment," he repeated.

"If you want to pull a Gene Kelly on the rainy streets of Denver," she said with more than a hint of cynicism, "don't let me stop you. Please. Be my guest."

With disconcerting ease he returned his focus—and his orthodontic dream of a smile—back to Jennifer. "Has anyone ever told you that you look like Lauren Bacall?"

"Oh, please." She rolled her eyes.

"You do," he insisted. "Same cool, ironic twist to the lips. Same diffident posture."

"Maybe it's my padded shoulders," she said, warming to him in spite of her reservations. "This is a vintage suit from the forties."

"It's perfect. You remind me of the way she looked in *To Have and Have Not*. The young Lauren Bacall."

"Young?" Jennifer grinned. "I'm thirty-one."

"Must be the light."

As he glanced up at the neon sign, she studied him more closely. Though his regimental striped tie was loosened, his navy-blue business suit was neat and well fitted—probably expensive—and he carried a leather briefcase. Apart from that roguish smile, he appeared to be quite conservative. And mysteriously familiar.

Jennifer heard herself asking one of those clichéd questions that were better left to old movies or singles' bars. "Have we met before?"

"Ever do business with Continental National Bank?"

"Have I ever!" Her feelings for Continental were a combination of deep gratitude and the prickle of resentment that came every month when her loan payment fell due. Two years ago Continental had financed the opening of her arts and crafts shop, Watt's Up. More recently she had arranged an art show for their lobby, using some of the better stained-glass pieces from her own shop and some original watercolors, including a few of her own.

She visualized the neutral colors of the bank, the marbleized, streamlined counter for the tellers and the neat rows of desks. With a mental jolt the pieces clicked into place. "I saw you in a meeting with Mr. Sanders, my business loan officer."

"Sanders? You're Watt's Up. Jennifer Watt, isn't it?"

"It is. And you're…"

"David Constable."

"Really? I've heard a lot about you from Beth Andrews. She truly appreciates your efforts on her behalf."

Though the downpour showed no sign of abatement, Jennifer was no longer anxious to flee to her van. David Constable, she repeated to herself. What a nice, stable, solid name! He wasn't some sort of midnight marauder. He was a banker.

"Beth used you for a reference," he said. "And you were pointed out to me while you were setting up the art show in the lobby. I should have introduced myself at that time."

"It's just as well that you didn't." The transporting and hanging of stained glass had been a nightmare. By the time the last piece was carefully placed to catch the available light, Jennifer's usually neat business attire had been discarded in favor of jeans and a T-shirt. Besides, she thought, meeting at midnight under a neon marquee was much more romantic.

"I can't quite believe it," she said. "You don't seem like a banker."

"Oh?" He gave her a one-eyebrow-raised look, like the one that Jimmy Stewart did so well. "What are bankers supposed to seem like?"

"I don't mean to be presumptuous or rude," she said. "I just don't expect to find vice presidents from Continental National at midnight movie festivals. Seems an odd hobby."

"Does it? Well, I suppose you're right." He feigned deep thought. "I don't believe I've encountered another banker tonight. Nor have I met bankers at the mass media courses I've taken. Nor at the Telluride Film Festival. Nor at any of the film production seminars I've attended."

Properly chastised, Jennifer mumbled, "Touché."

"I hope you don't think I'm being forward," he said, "but would you consider sharing an umbrella?"

She stared at him as though he'd just offered her a priceless treasure. "Do you have one?"

"Of course. We banker types always think ahead." He flipped open his briefcase. With a flourish he produced a small collapsible umbrella and popped it open. "Amortization. Insurance. Fluctuating interest rates. And I read the weather reports this morning."

She mentally applauded this evidence of foresight. "I'm parked four blocks away," she warned.

"Better than me. I'm not even parked. I had planned to stop by the office and then catch a bus."

"Then it's settled. You give me a dry walk to the car, and I'll give you a ride home."

"It's a deal. Ready?"

"Not quite." Jennifer's slim skirt wasn't made for dashing and leaping over puddles. Starting at the hem, she unbuttoned it to a point well above her knees. The slash provided wide mobility for her long legs.

"A convertible," David commented.

"No, that's when you take the top down." Without thinking she adjusted the collar of his jacket. "But don't get any ideas."

"Too late," he said.

His astute attention to her unbuttoning process gave her an unexpected twinge of pleasure. *Fancy that, even bankers have hormones*, she thought. "Ready," she announced, looking regretfully at her high-heeled, strappy sandals. "Wish I'd brought my Reeboks."

"Lauren Bacall would never wear Reeboks."

As they ventured out into the driving rain, Jennifer once again felt like humming. To keep from getting wet, she snuggled close to David, finding warm shelter against the storm. Their proximity, she thought, was marvelous. It would be easy to develop an intimacy with this surprising banker.

Her foot splashed in a puddle, and she let out a yelp.

"Maybe I should carry you," he offered.

"Don't be silly." She couldn't resist a little dig. "I didn't think vice presidents were ever silly."

"And I thought artists were impulsive enough to march bare-headed through the rain."

They darted into the entryway of a jewelry store on the corner and stood there gazing out at the city street through a curtain of rain.

"Artists *are* impulsive," she informed him. "But I'm a retailer, remember?"

"Not true. Your signature was on a couple of the watercolor sketches in the art show at Continental. I almost bought one. A portrait of an old cowboy."

"Really?" She beamed. Her artist friends usually dismissed Jennifer's work as being too sentimental. "Anyway, painting is just my hobby," she said. "Not my life."

"I don't believe it." He lapsed into a Humphrey Bogart impersonation. "And I can read you like a book, sweetheart."

"That was pitiful."

"Couldn't help myself." He shrugged. "Bogey seemed appropriate. I've always admired his way with women."

"Is that why you like classic movies? A chance to brush up on technique?"

"First, you tell me about Jennifer Watt the artist."

"That's history," she said firmly. "Two years ago I opened Watt's Up and everything changed. I had to keep track of inventories and come up with advertising plans and pay off loans. And guess what? I discovered that I enjoyed being responsible."

"Doesn't the store make you feel tied down?"

"Occasionally." She combed her fingers through her hair. The thick humidity made the straight blond tendrils hang heavily against her nape. "I don't often get away."

"Because the store can't run without you?" he asked.

"Of course not. I have two capable part-time clerks. And Beth Andrews sometimes gives me a hand."

"Then why?" he prodded. "Why can't you leave the store while someone else takes care of your business?"

"I don't have anywhere I want to go," she blurted out. As she heard herself speak, the statement surprised her. Where had that feeling come from? And why did her words seem so pathetic and lonely? She certainly didn't think of herself as a sorry old maid with no place to go. "I didn't mean that the way it sounded."

He gave her that disbelieving, one-eyebrow-raised look.

"Really," she protested. "I'm not whining. I hate whiners. And I've already done New York and London and the Louvre."

His eyebrow rose even higher. "This topic bears further discussion. Over a cup of coffee?"

It was her turn to be skeptical. Hot, steaming coffee sounded wonderful but impossible. "Even a well-prepared guy like you can't order up a coffee shop that's nearby and open."

"Trust me."

"If you can find coffee, I'll drink it."

He handed her his umbrella and briefcase. Without further explanation he scooped her up in his arms and charged out into the street.

"David! Put me down!"

"Not until I find coffee."

Laughing and bouncing, she threw one arm around his shoulders for balance. No matter how she positioned the umbrella, her legs were getting drenched. "You're crazy."

"Coffee, coffee, where's the coffee?"

He upped his pace to a steady gallop, and she jostled wildly against him. Cold, fresh rain splattered her face, and she gasped with laughter.

Struggling one-handed with the umbrella, Jennifer brought it down over both their heads.

"Hey," he yelled. "I can't see."

She flipped the umbrella back. It was totally ineffective in providing shelter. "Better?"

"Great."

"But we're all wet!"

Bobbling up and down in his arms, she felt foolish and ridiculous and happier than she'd been in years. She was giggling. The responsible retailer, Jennifer Watt, was actually tittering like a schoolgirl.

As he took a wide leap over a puddle, she let out a loud whoop of laughter. What a night! What a ride! Who could have thought that a staid banker from Continental National was capable of such nonsense?

David dodged into the entryway of a men's accessories shop and dropped her legs with a thump. Through his heavy breathing he was laughing, too.

She leaned against him in the tiny doorway, weak from laughter and the effort of holding the umbrella over them. His chest heaved against her as he drew another deep breath. His arm was still around her, encircling her waist.

In the small alcove they were close. Very close. Too close. But Jennifer didn't care. She'd thrown caution to the winds—rather, to the rains. She shivered against him as the lengths of their bodies met through the sodden barriers of their damp clothing.

"You're cold," he said.

"And wet," she concurred. "But no more than you."

She reached up to brush a droplet of rain from his forehead—a useless exercise since he was thoroughly rain soaked, his hair slicked down against his head. She looked up at him and began laughing again. "Oh, David. Your ears."

"Now you know my worst secret—ears like Dumbo."

"Not at all." She tried to stifle her chuckles. "It makes you look more like Clark Gable."

"Frankly, my dear, I don't give a damn."

"Poor Gable. You're all wet."

"It doesn't matter." His lips curved in an ironic variation of his gorgeous smile. "This suit is drip-dry."

She shivered again. "So where's this promised coffee?"

He pointed toward Continental National Bank right across the street. "Third floor, employees' lounge."

Before she could object, he grabbed her hand and dragged her across the deserted, rain-slick street to the wide concrete portico at the front entrance to the bank.

"Watch this, sweetheart," he lisped like Bogart as he tapped at a metal strip beside the glass doors. "I got to do this just right, or else the alarms go off. And the coppers will be here before you can say, *The Maltese Falcon*." He tapped again and shouted, "George! Hey, George Dooley! Yo, it's me."

From inside the dimly lighted building Jennifer saw a movement—nothing distinct, but a sort of shuffling of the shadows inside the foyer. Then George appeared. He squinted out the door, rubbed his eyes and yawned. Though he wore a pistol strapped around his formidable girth, the night watchman was about as threatening as an old sheepdog. He used four different keys to open the door.

"Evening, Mr. Constable. Thought you was going to be here at midnight on the nose. And who's the lady?"

"My associate." David hustled her through the doors.

"I need a name," George said as he relocked the doors carefully. "I've got to log you in on my nightly reports."

"Lauren Bacall," Jennifer quickly replied. She didn't want her real name listed as an after-midnight visitor to the bank where she did business.

George looked at her and scratched his head. He seemed puzzled, as if something were wrong but he didn't know what.

Jennifer didn't want to wait around until he figured it out. She scurried into the elevator beside David and tried to look respectable until the doors whooshed shut. "I can't believe you did this to me, David. I have a reputation to maintain."

"Come on, 'Miz Bacall.' Haven't you ever wanted to be inside a bank after closing? Just you and me and all that green money?"

"And George," she reminded him.

"Besides, I promised you coffee, and I'm a guy who delivers on his promises."

On the third floor he led her down a bland white hallway, past several offices and into the employees' lounge, where he flicked on the overhead fluorescents to reveal several white Formica tables with matching plastic chairs and a row of vending machines lined up along one wall.

David went directly to the coffee machine. "What'll it be? Cream? Sugar?"

"I'll take it straight."

"Anything else? I can offer you gooey, stale pastry. Or canned macaroni and cheese. Or—my favorite—half-melted candy bars."

She briefly considered the selection of almost every preservative known to man and shook her head. "Not that I object to junk food, but I've just eaten a ton of popcorn and jujubes."

While the coffee gushed into a paper cup, he escorted her to one of the tables and pulled out her chair. In response to his courtly gesture she sat delicately, positioning herself to keep her high-slit skirt from gaping immodestly.

"So, Jennifer, what got you interested in old movies?"

"Late-night television," she said. "I used to lose track of time while I was painting. Then it would be after midnight and I'd be too excited to sleep. At first I was selective—only *The Thin Man* movies and anything with Katharine Hepburn. Then I developed an interest in musicals. Then those *Dracula* movies. Then everything else." She patted herself on one padded shoulder. "And I love forties costumes."

"Speaking of which." He peeled off his suit coat and draped it over the back of one of the chairs. "This is a good time to dry out."

It didn't surprise Jennifer to see that he was broad-shouldered and lean beneath his jacket. Probably well muscled, she thought. He'd make an excellent artist's model. He tugged off his tie and rolled up his sleeves to reveal strong wrists.

With an odd self-consciousness she removed her own damp jacket. Her lightweight peplum blouse seemed too sheer for Continental National Bank and much too revealing.

"Old-fashioned blouse to go with the suit?" he asked.

She nodded. She'd purchased the blouse and several other choice items from a going-out-of-business sale at an old costume shop on Larimer Street.

He whistled his appreciation. "It's beautiful."

Far too sheer, she decided. But her vulnerability wasn't limited to the blouse. A suit of armor couldn't protect her from her own internal response to David's direct approval. Though her stomach was doing a tango, she tried for a cool, conversational tone as she sipped her coffee. "How did you get interested in movies?"

"What can I say? Maybe it's inherited, like my ears and my eyebrows. Clayton Forbes was my uncle."

"Who?"

"Clayton Forbes, the all-American Wasp Man. You remember, don't you? It was a television series in the mid- to late fifties." He made his fingers into a trumpet, blasted five discordant notes and deepened his voice to a dramatic pitch. "Wasp Man. He flies. He soars on silver wing. Men of evil, beware his sting."

"Cute," Jennifer said. "But a little before my time."

"Not into TV reruns, eh? He was also in a couple of Harriet Kelton's early films, but they were real forgettable."

"Harriet Kelton?" A wave of nostalgia swept over Jennifer. She remembered Miss Kelton. She even remembered the sequined green gown she had worn in one of her few Technicolor movies. "Wasn't she beautiful! Did you know that she lives around here, someplace in the mountains?"

"At The Lodge near Conifer."

"You've met her?"

"Yeah, she and my uncle stayed in contact. He even found a couple of parts for her on *Wasp Man*."

"Found?" Jennifer bristled. "Harriet Kelton was a star. She could pick and choose."

"At one time she could. But that time was forty years ago."

How sad! Perky, pretty Harriet Kelton must be in her seventies, Jennifer thought. It was hard to imagine. For people like Jennifer the waning stars never fell. Since she didn't read movie magazines or follow careers, her heroes and heroines existed only on celluloid, a medium that didn't show wrinkles or bodily sags.

Wouldn't it be nice, she thought, if real life could be managed the same way, if the past could be neatly recorded and filed away only to be viewed in splendid, clear moments? But maybe not. Jennifer had several dismal memories she'd like to suppress forever, like bad B-grade movies.

There was the con man who posed as an art promoter and lured her to nonexistent artistic fame and fortune in Santa Fe, New Mexico.

Then there was that cruel review by an art critic with an ax to grind when it came to female artists in the Southwest. "Another callow lass," he'd said, "who wants to be Georgia O'Keeffe when she grows up." Even after Jennifer saw four more reviews written by the same man that said essentially the same thing, she was convinced that her own work was substandard.

And her parents' disapproval. Her inner melodrama ground to a tragic halt. Only three years ago her mother and father had passed away. With a physical start she shoved away that painful sorrow.

She would never hear their gentle words of reconciliation, never feel the warmth of her mom's embrace, never hear Dad's rich baritone singing hymns with the church choir. And they would never have the satisfaction of seeing their only daughter behave the way they'd begged her to for so long—like a responsible member of society. A retailer, not an artist.

"Jennifer?" David's deep voice intruded.

"Just feeling my age," she said softly. "And wishing that memories could be recorded over as easily as videotapes."

"Interesting philosophy."

Though his tone remained light, David wanted urgently to know more about Jennifer Watt—her sorrows and her joys. He wanted a complete biography, photographs, videotapes, old report cards, everything. Damn, there was so little time.

"What memories would you erase?" he asked.

"The usual. Certain moments from my girlhood in Ohio that I'd like to record over. And there's a nasty art critic I'd like to rub out. And a swindling art promoter."

"My God, woman. You're bloodthirsty."

"It's only what they deserve," she said cheerily. "Take that slime-bag art promoter. He took the life savings of ten local artists, conned four of us into going to Santa Fe and then disappeared. I had twenty dollars in my pocket and had to work in a Mexican restaurant until I raised plane fare. The end result is that I hate tacos. And people who run out on me."

David watched the subtle misting in her clear blue eyes before she recovered her cool, sardonic gaze. This small variation in her expression spoke more to him than her words. He saw a woman who had been innocently credulous. Betrayal had turned her trust to pain. She'd been hurt. And she hated people who ran out on her. How would she feel about him?

"One of life's little lessons," she said. "I learned to despise people who prey on the dreams of artists. I'm very careful in my shop to be honest with my artist suppliers and to treat them with the respect they deserve."

"I have this sneaky hunch, Jennifer, that you would have been honest without a lesson from a con man."

"Banker's judgment?"

"Human intuition." He finished his coffee and reached across the Formica table to touch her hand. "Jennifer Watt, why didn't I meet you sooner?"

"Bad timing?"

"The worst."

In the depths of his smoky-gray eyes she found a tenderness and sensitivity that should have been puzzling. They'd met less than an hour ago, but Jennifer knew that her own eyes were reflections of his. She liked David, liked him very well. He was handsome, charmingly silly and interesting. Though she'd teased him about his profession, she appreciated the stability and responsibility required of a banker.

"You were right," she said. "There is something sexy about a bank after dark."

"Are you finished your coffee?"

She nodded. "How do they keep the money? Is it all piled up like leaves in autumn?"

"Right, Jen," he said sarcastically. "Want a limited tour?"

"Can I touch the money?"

"No, Jennifer. You'll have to settle for desk phones and file cabinets."

He took her hand and escorted her to the exit of the employees' lounge. As they strolled along the sterile, windowless hallway to the elevator, he offered a humorous monologue on his seven years at Continental National and his rise from the lower echelons—and lower floors—to vice presidency on the ninth floor. "Bankers," he explained, "are reverent with money. Only people like my Uncle Clayton keep loose cash to roll around in."

They entered the elevator, and she turned to him. "So tell me about Uncle Wasp Man."

"The fact is that Clayton Forbes was a fairly decent actor." David shrugged. "He was also a fairly strange human being."

"Runs in the family, does it?"

"After the series folded, he retired to his Malibu Beach house and lived like a hermit. I've heard he only came out after dark. Some people say he dressed only in his silver cape, and I can't tell you they're wrong. Anyway, he died a few months ago."

"I'm sorry, David."

"Me, too. He was really special. When I was six years old, I visited him during the summer. It was great. He took me to watch the series being filmed. After he retired, that changed. We didn't see each other much after that."

Jennifer wasn't quite sure what to say, so she remained silent, watching David's expressive face.

"Good old Wasp Man," he mused, holding the elevator door for her and raising his hand in salute. "Beware his sting."

"Guess I don't have to worry," she said. "That only applies to men of evil, doesn't it?"

"Ah, Jennifer. There's always a sting." He took her hand and led her down the hall. "I'm feeling one right now."

"Are you sure it's not rain dripping into your shorts?"

Though he smiled, she sensed that David was tense. Apparently he attached great significance to the tale of Wasp Man and his fabled stinger. Why? Was it a family secret?

Jennifer dismissed her wonderings. David's past and his family could be the topic of countless future conversations. She felt certain that they would see each other again. They would have plenty of time to learn all about each other.

He stopped at an oak door bearing his nameplate and plugged his key into the lock. "Before I show you my office, I'd like to ask you out for dinner tomorrow night. At six o'clock?"

"Maybe I should wait to see what's behind door number one."

"Dinner? I promise it won't be tacos."

"Thank you, I'd like very much to see you again."

Gently he took her hand and led her into his office. Through the uncurtained windows she could see the thunderstorm continuing unabated. Lightning clawed the dark sky and rainfall obscured the twinkling city lights.

"It's fantastic," she said. "Don't turn on the light."

As they stood together in his dark office, watching, Jennifer felt an acute sense of anticipation. There was something special about her meeting with David. As surely as thunder came with rain, she knew there would be other nights for them—crimson twilights and snowy winter nights when the skies were as blank as a fresh slate.

The electricity of the storm jumped into her heart as David's hand eased up her arm. She could feel his nearness and smell the mustiness of their damp clothing.

Perhaps this was too sudden. Too rushed. But Jennifer was old enough, wise enough, to listen to her own bodily intuition. With every pore her body assured her that his timing was perfect. This moment was inevitable. Her moistened lips parted in invitation as she melted into his arms.

When they kissed, Jennifer felt the static energy of the storm, jagged and wild within her. An achingly sweet excitement crashed and surged around them and through them.

His firm, strong body felt exactly right against hers. Their embrace was everything it should be—warm and gentle yet taut with excitement. Unheard thunder seemed to echo within her.

His breath tickled her ear as he murmured, "I should have met you years ago."

"There's time for us, David. Plenty of time."

He reached for the light switch. Overhead the fluorescents flared, and Jennifer blinked. Then blinked again.

She picked up the nameplate on the desk. David Constable. His office. There were cardboard boxes half packed on the desk and the floor. All the personal touches had been dismantled or removed.

"I don't understand," she said.

"Tomorrow is my last day."

"You've been promoted to a higher floor?"

He shook his head. His eyes were averted, and Jennifer felt a sharp pang of dismay. He was leaving. Before they could fulfill the promise of the shared nights and sunrises, he was going away. She'd only known him for an hour, but her sense of abandonment felt ancient and painful.

Maybe not. She hoped against the odds. "Another job?"

"Another life, Jennifer. I'm moving to Malibu Beach in ten days."

# 2

TEN DAYS PASSED in a kinescopic flash. They shared champagne by candlelight and French bread from a picnic basket. He escorted her along a steep, rocky mountain path to a shimmering waterfall, and she took him roller-skating in Cheesman Park. They picked colorful bouquets of wildflowers, and she took possession of the blooming cactus from his condo. They packed and garage-saled David's belongings, except for the *Adam's Rib* poster and the framed autograph from Cary Grant, both of which Jennifer claimed for her own.

In ten short days they played a lifetime of memories for Jennifer's private inner video recorder. They shared so much, laughed so often. They waltzed in the moonlight and ran hand in hand through sunlit fields of columbine.

For ten days Jennifer had put off thinking about their future. She'd wished it away, pretending that it wouldn't happen. Inevitably the future became the present.

It wasn't until she dropped him off at Stapleton Airport that the truth sank in. He was gone. He had left her.

On the drive home she decided that David's midlife crisis was driving her crazy. That's what it was—a midlife crisis. Why else would he quit a perfectly good job? He had a career as a vice president at a downtown bank. How could he want to be a Hollywood movie producer?

She squeezed her van into a parking space on the street in front of her Victorian-style home, slammed the door and stomped up the steps. Who did he think he was? Paul Gauguin, the impressionist artist who dumped wife, kids and stable career to take off for Tahiti?

She unlocked her front door and steamed inside. It wasn't fair. David had no right to be so impulsive. Tomorrow he would "take a meeting" with some half-baked production company executives. At the pink and palm-tree paradise of the Beverly Hills Hotel.

She stalked across her bedroom and flung open the door to her walk-in closet. No more time to think about David Constable. She'd scheduled a cocktail party for several of the artists who supplied Watt's Up with their work. Her guests would be arriving soon. Time to get on with life.

That was what she told herself as she stared into her closet. Yet her vision blurred the variety of colors into a pastel-dominated montage as her mind focused on the scene at the airport terminal where she'd dropped him off at the curb only half an hour before. At least she'd done that well. She'd left quickly enough to avoid an embarrassing farewell scene.

"I should never have agreed to see him after that first night," she told the jumble of shoes on her closet floor. "You're a real sucker, Jennifer. Really dumb."

She reached blindly into the row of clothing and pulled out a pale green sundress. It was the dress she'd worn on the day David came by Watt's Up and convinced her to play hooky. They'd gone to the mountains and waded in a deliciously cold stream.

An angry breath puffed through her lips as she jammed the dress back into the closet. "I should have drowned him in Clear Creek."

She'd tried to convince him that all he needed was a vacation. If he was so determined to become a feature film producer, he could have gone to Cannes to check out the action. Or back to the Telluride Film Festival. But noooo, that wasn't enough. He had to give up everything: quit his job, sell his car, sublease his condo and give away his Boston fern.

Jennifer flopped down on her bed. Damn him! She couldn't decide if she was more angry that he was leaving or that she couldn't go with him.

She glanced at the mauve decorator phone beside her bed. What if he called right now? His plane wasn't due to take off for another half hour. What if he called right now and asked her—for the ten millionth time—to go with him?

In her heart she yearned to fly away with David, to weave a fabric of dreams, to laugh and run with him along the Pacific shore. But right now it was impossible.

Tomorrow was Saturday—the first day of the Labor Day long weekend, the first day of the Third Annual Denver Arts and Crafts Fair. Jennifer's shop would, of course, be represented. Although she'd scheduled several workers to man the Watt's Up booth and had already selected and designed the displays, Jennifer knew she had to be there. She couldn't take a chance on a screwup. Last year she'd grossed seven thousand dollars in three days. A very pretty penny, she thought, for a small shop specializing in stained glass, original artworks and pottery. The receipts from this weekend alone could be enough to carry her into the Christmas season.

She sighed. Maybe in a week she could catch a plane to Los Angeles. That thought consoled her. Surely she could last seven days without David. Lots of other couples carried on successful long-distance relationships.

Were they a couple? She'd only known him for ten days. They hadn't even made love. Jennifer pondered for a moment, trying to come up with a word or a phrase that described her whirlwind relationship with David.

A physical attraction? That sounded so clinical. Certainly she had been attracted to him from the moment she laid eyes on him, but that wasn't it.

An infatuation? Jennifer wrinkled her nose. Infatuations were for adolescents. She was thirty-one. He was thirty-five. They were well into adulthood.

Courtship was too old-fashioned.

Commitment wasn't accurate. They hadn't exchanged promises.

Jennifer gazed up at the antique fixture on the ceiling. What would David call it? What would he want their relationship to be? She had the phrase—romantic understanding. Someday, somewhere, someway, she knew they would be together.

"Good grief, I'm beginning to sound like an old movie."

She returned to her closet, determined to make the best of this frustrating situation. Deliberately she selected a sleeveless, bright red satiny dress with spaghetti straps and a plunging neckline. The soft material glided over her body, fitting snugly around her slim hips and flaring to fullness around her knees.

*This is more like it*, she thought. *If he's going to act like an irresponsible idiot, I'll dress like a heartless vamp.*

The telephone on the bedside table rang only once before she grabbed the receiver. "Hello?"

"Come away wiz me to zee Casbah, and we will make beautiful music together."

"Wrong number, Sinbad. This is not the harem."

"It's not?"

"Not a veil nor a eunuch in sight."

"I knew that, sweetheart." David slipped easily into his tough-guy Bogart impression. "The young Lauren Bacall would never be a harem girl. I was trying to put one over on you, kid."

Through the background noise of the airport crowds, pagings and static, his voice sounded very near. Why did he have to leave?

"I was checking my suitcases," he said, lapsing into his normal baritone, "and I realized that there's something very important that I left behind."

"What's that?"

"You."

"Me?" she yelped as she balanced, storklike, on one leg, wriggling into a pair of red panty hose. "I don't appreciate being compared to a piece of luggage, David."

"In that case, I'll find you a first-class seat. With complimentary champagne? A first-run movie?" He paused. "Anything. I'll promise anything, Jennifer, if you'll come with me. Just for a couple of days."

"I have to get through the craft fair. Then we'll see."

"At least come back to the airport. There's been a delay, and my plane won't leave for an hour. We could have a classic farewell scene. Like Bogart and Bergman in *Casablanca*."

"Ingrid was the one flying away," she corrected. "And it was a prop plane, and foggier than it ever gets in Denver. And they were never going to see each other again."

"It's the sentiment that counts," he said. "I want my chance to be noble and brave like Bogey."

"This isn't wartime, David. And you're not escaping the Nazi menace. You're moving to Malibu Beach."

"Are you jealous? Or just mad."

"Me? Mad? Hah!"

"Jealous?" he repeated.

"Of what? An irresponsible attitude?"

"Freedom."

"Foolishness."

"Right you are, Jennifer Watt. Can't you see it on a movie marquee? He *is* foolish. He *is* irresponsible and unpredictable. He *is* David Constable."

"Have you got a title for this epic?"

"How about *Sleeping Late*? Or *Sand Between His Toes*?"

"I hate to admit it," she said. "But it sounds wonderful."

No doubt about it, she thought with a shudder, David had disrupted her former contentment with her retail shop. His pursuit of an exciting, creative career had awakened her own artistic impulsiveness. In daydreams her memories of her irresponsible youth when she'd lived without schedules seemed sweet and happy. She yearned to travel, to follow whichever star burned brightest on the uncharted horizon.

But she also liked to eat.

"Come with me, Jennifer."

"That's a mighty seductive proposition, sir." She stretched the phone cord toward the closet and grabbed a pair of patent leather pumps. "But wouldn't I get in the way? I thought part of this journey was an attempt to find the real David Constable."

"Nobody ever said I had to do it alone. Please, Jennifer."

"Why don't you stay here? It's a much more sensible solution."

"You know why." She heard him clear his throat. "I'd be crazy to pass up such a great opportunity. Who would have thought that my Uncle Wasp Man would have left me his beach house and all its contents?"

"You could sell the house," she suggested. "Beachfront property in Malibu Beach must be worth a fortune."

"I want to invest in myself. If this doesn't work after a year, I'll come back. My three-piece suits will still fit, and I'll have the satisfaction of knowing that I tried. Won't you give me a proper send-off? I'll buy all the cappuccino you can drink if you'll come with me for the weekend."

"I have responsibilities here."

"Tell you what. Come back to the airport and we'll revise the *Casablanca* farewell to include a long, passionate kiss."

"I can't." She fished her lipstick out of her purse and blindly applied a fresh coat of bright red to match her dress. "No when I have twelve guests who will be here in approximately two minutes."

"Cocktails with a bunch of artists. You'd choose them over me? Where's your sense of romance, lady?"

"Buried beneath my sense of survival. Besides, I need to plan with these people for the Christmas season," she reminded him. "I want to make sure we have enough of the big sellers in stock. And no inappropriate pieces."

"I've heard about those inappropriate ones," he said. "I seem to remember your loan officer mentioning a strange memo about two gross of green-and-red neon tongues from Delilah."

"She's the exception, and I allow her a lot of leeway because she's a creative genius. Everybody else is pretty much on target with salable items." She paused. "I can't leave town right now, David."

"All of a sudden I don't want to go. I'd rather stay here and listen to you discussing art with Delilah. I have this foolish, unpredictable urge to hang around your shop, watch you dusting the handmade hobbyhorses and shining up the stained glass. We'd go out for chocolate croissants. Maybe take a walk. It's going to be autumn soon, and I won't see the leaves changing. I'll be in Malibu Beach with palm trees and balmy breezes."

"Poor baby," she said unsympathetically.

"I want to see you in wintertime, Jennifer. In a white furry parka. I want to taste the first snowflakes of winter on your lips."

His usual ebullience seemed to dissipate as she listened. He spoke of autumn and winter, seasons they had never shared, and she felt a chill along her spine.

"Jennifer? What I'm trying to say is that I care about you. A lot. I like being around you. I like the way you laugh. The way you look. Your perfume. I even like the way you snuffle and blow your nose in old movies."

She sank onto the bed, unable to answer. She tried to cling to her anger, tried not to mourn his departure. But her rage was gone. She felt weak and sad. Her eyelids ached with unshed tears.

"I'm going to miss you, lady. Miss you like hell."

"I'll miss you, David," she murmured as the doorbell rang.

"Here's looking at you, kid. Take care of yourself."

The telephone went dead, and Jennifer longed for the luxury of tears. "Oh, God," she whispered as the doorbell chimed again. "This is going to be the worst night of my life."

Later she would cry. Right now there was nothing she could do about David's absence but try to forget. And to adjust.

In jerky movements she forced herself to stand. Her body responded unwillingly. Thoughts of David filled her mind, leaving no room for simple physical commands. Her knees felt disconnected from the rest of her long legs, and the distance from the bedroom to the front door seemed like twenty miles. She walked slowly, using each step to compose herself.

A gawky bearded man stood waiting, and Jennifer inwardly cringed. Why did it have to be Philo Andrews? He was the one person who was sure to give her a hard time.

He stared at her satiny dress and drawled, "Don't you think the red is a bit obvious?"

"Nice to see you, too."

Despite his disheveled appearance Philo was a commercial cameraman who made a decent living from work on industrial films and TV ads. Unfortunately, he fancied himself a feature film cinematographer, and his frustration made him aggressively cynical. Jennifer probably would have avoided him except that his wife, Beth, was one of her best friends. Every year Beth and Jennifer produced a popular line of

Christmas cards and calendars using Beth's poetry and Jennifer's watercolor sketches.

Philo handed her a bottle of white wine and sauntered into the high-ceilinged, gracious parlor. His gangly strides reminded Jennifer of a scarecrow on stilts. "About the red," he said, whirling to face her. "It's camouflage. You're trying to hide the way you feel about what's-his-name."

"Are you referring to David?"

"None other. The banker who swept you off your conscientious little tootsies. Has he left yet?"

"He just called from the airport."

"And you, Jennifer, are miserable." He straddled the piano bench and began playing with the long fringe of an antique shawl that draped over the spinet's rosewood surface. "You got it bad, babe. Old Philo can tell."

"In the first place, I am not in misery," she snapped. "Second, I have known Mr. Constable only ten days—not long enough to 'have it bad.' Third, don't you ever call me 'babe' again."

"Beth told me you'd be in a bad mood," he said, complacently stroking his beard.

"You have two choices, Philo. Either you can sit around gloating about my obvious red. Or you can do me a favor. Something useful."

"Name it."

"Would you tend the bar for me?"

"Sure thing. I tend to go heavy on the booze, so nobody ever complains." He stepped behind the portable bar and began checking her liquor stock. "Now that your latest flame is gone, would you go out with an old buddy of mine from Sacramento?"

"No, thanks." Her response was automatic. The last time Philo and Beth had fixed her up with a blind date, the man had all the charm of an unwashed orangutan. Besides, she couldn't begin to think about dating. Not when the man she'd cast as Mr. Right was preparing to disappear into the sunset.

She wondered if David felt the same way about her. Jennifer frowned. The thought of his dating other women really rattled her. Would he be enjoying himself with nubile starlets while she pursued the glum life of a workaholic?

They should have made a pact, she thought, like in the movies. They should have promised to rendezvous in one year at the Empire State Building, and at the end of the year he would be running across the street and he would be struck down by a taxi and...

"Hey, you. Lady in red. Where's the vodka?"

"What?" She exchanged the faded dreams of what might have been for blunt reality.

"Vodka. It's a clear liquid."

She picked through the bottles on the marble countertop. "Here it is. Would you mix me something?"

"A screwdriver," he said. "That's Beth's drink."

"Where is Beth?"

"She had one of those political things where she's doing the brochures and video for the candidate." He poured a generous amount of vodka and added a splash of orange juice. "But she'll be here later, and you can cry on her shoulder."

The doorbell rang. Before Jennifer could excuse herself and answer it, Philo reached across the bar and touched her shoulder. "Jennifer," he said in an unusually gentle voice. "You are okay, aren't you?"

"Please don't be sympathetic, Philo." She tried to be flip but couldn't prevent a small quaver. "I don't think my system could stand the shock."

"I don't like seeing you hurt." His sardonic grin reappeared, giving the lie to his brief show of humanity. "So if you want me to put out a hit on this ex-banker character, I'd be glad to."

"I think that's the nicest thing you've ever said to me."

The doorbell clanged again, and she went to answer it.

The other guests arrived in rapid succession—Delilah, several potters, a wood-carver who specialized in beautiful elfin figures, a glassblower and a Navajo woman named Laughing Turtle.

Jennifer didn't have to work too hard to be a good hostess. With the genial group that task was easy. As long as the food trays were stacked high with cold cuts, crudités, breads and dips, her colleagues and friends were happy. Philo's heavy hand as bartender encouraged the vivacious flow of conversation.

When the room had filled, Jennifer climbed onto a kitchen stool and called for attention. "Everybody listen."

"What did I tell you?" Philo cheerfully teased. "There's no free lunch."

"Absolutely right," she responded. She wanted to get the business out of the way as quickly and painlessly as possible. "Those of you who have signed up to help at the craft fair, be there tomorrow morning at eight."

One of the potters groaned. "Eight o'clock?"

"In the morning," Jennifer emphasized. While she had their attention, she hurried on to other business. "One more thing. Ladies and gentlemen, Christmas is coming. I must talk privately with each of you so we can decide what to stock. Please try to remember what sold well last year."

"Baubles, bangles and beads," recalled a silversmith. "Anything priced under ten bucks."

"Too true," trilled Delilah of the neon tongues. "The general public has no soul, no depth of appreciation."

"The general public," said Jennifer loudly before she lost control of her audience, "the general public is just like you and me. They have twenty Christmas presents to buy and only twenty-five dollars to spend. Let's try to make it easy for them to stretch their budget, to find a nice gift for Aunt Minnie in Kansas. And something exotic for the punk nephew in San Francisco."

"Yes," Laughing Turtle piped up, "but we must also be prepared with expensive items. Last year I sold many silver squash blossom necklaces."

"I did okay, too," said a potter. "Four orders for custom dinnerware and chalices."

"Contact me before November so we can make some decisions," Jennifer concluded as shoptalk began to take over. "That's all the business for this evening. Enjoy."

She hopped down from her makeshift podium and replenished her drink. Her easygoing style of doing business depended primarily on good will between the suppliers and her shop, and she usually dispensed a vast amount of honest, friendly encouragement. Tonight she wasn't in the mood. Tonight she wanted to be like Garbo. Alone.

That wish was not to be. Clyde Theodopolous, a heavyset bear of a man who ironically specialized in intricate glassblowing, settled comfortably at the spinet with an air that said he intended to stay there until dawn. He banged out old favorites while Laughing Turtle and Delilah sang along in perfect harmony.

In spite of her depression, Jennifer grinned when the duo forgot the words to "Daisy" and made up their own version. She enjoyed being around these professional artists. No matter how much she complained about their moods and the frequent inability to meet deadlines, she appreciated their creativity and skill. And they usually made her feel cheerful and positive.

Maybe life wasn't so dreadful, she thought. If she could still smile, there was hope. Picking up an empty food tray and clutching her cocktail glass, Jennifer headed toward the kitchen. Her intention was to refill the platter, but as soon as she was behind the swinging door, she plunked herself down on a stool. The room seemed to be spinning. How much had she had to drink?

With careful deliberation she peered at the clock on the microwave. Only a few minutes past eight. David's plane had undoubtedly taken off by now. He was gone.

Beth Andrews pushed through the swinging door into the kitchen. "What possessed you to use Philo as a bartender?" she greeted Jennifer.

"He's doing a swell job." Jennifer raised her glass in welcome. "Aren't you going to comment on my obvious red?"

"How much have you had?"

"Much, much," Jennifer admitted.

"That's what I thought. How about some nice coffee?"

"I don't look drunk, do I?"

"You look fine." Beth bustled around the kitchen, measuring coffee into the percolator. "And I love your dress, Jennifer. The red matches your eyes."

"Very funny. So how was the political thing?"

"Boring. I'm doing the brochures for a woman who is running for the Adams County Sewer Board. What do you think of this for a slogan: Waste Not, Want Not."

"Sounds messy."

"Sometimes I get fed up with my own commercialism. Philo says I should forget it all and let my creative juices flow."

"Sounds messier."

While Beth described the political meeting, Jennifer tried to concentrate, but her mind kept drifting away. Her eyes focused on the needlepoint picture hanging beside the wall phone. There's No Place Like Home, it said. Where was her home? On a jet headed for LAX. Why did he have to leave?

She jumped when Beth touched her arm. "Jennifer? Do you want to lie down for a while?"

"Nope. I'm a little down, but I'm not out. David was just another example of my uncanny ability to attach myself to the wrong Mr. Right. I have no reason to be upset."

"You don't have to play Superwoman for me. Why don't you go out to California and see him this weekend?"

"The weekend of the Labor Day craft fair? Get serious. Besides, if he wanted us to be together, he wouldn't have left."

"Is that fair?"

"No," Jennifer admitted. "But I don't want to be fair. Really, Beth, it's no big deal. I hardly even know the guy."

"But you care about him," Beth quietly concluded.

"Lust at first sight." She slumped down on a stool and rested her elbows on the countertop. "You'd think that at my age I'd know better. I'm too old for these stupid clichés."

"Tell me about when you first met," Beth prompted. "I know it was after that Classic Cinema Marathon."

"In the rain. There he stood with an umbrella, looking exactly like Clark Gable."

"Clark Gable? David doesn't have a mustache."

"His ears are funny, though."

"I never noticed."

"Take it from me," Jennifer said. "His ears are really strange in a cute sort of way."

"Cute? Somebody's who's over six feet tall and has shoulders like a longshoreman is cute?"

"He's got dimples, you know." Jennifer felt herself sinking to new depths of maudlin. "I should have proposed to him right on the spot. A formal wedding. He'd look great in a tux."

She paused, lost for a moment in memories. When she glanced at her silent friend, she saw kindness in Beth's eyes. "You're as bad as your husband," she said. "Except Philo is an unrepentant cynic and you're an incurable romantic."

"Don't you worry, Jennifer." Beth lightly touched her friend's shoulder. "He'll be back. And you'll be together. David is your destiny."

"Spoken like a poet," Jennifer said. "So let's talk about you. Still planning to buy your own printing equipment?"

"That certainly brings us back to harsh reality."

"Please, Beth. I'd rather think about something other than destiny right now. Tell me your plans."

"Nothing definite. I'm still fed up with the high cost of printing my brochures, and equipment seems so solid. After all, Philo has his cameras and lights. I deserve my own press." Beth exhaled a deep breath. "On the other hand, I don't really want to open a print shop. It seems so permanent. Do you ever regret settling down to a shop?"

"Sometimes."

"But you've done so well. Tell me all your magic secrets about leases and locations and tax laws and profit margins."

As they fell into a business discussion, Jennifer succeeded in putting her emotions on automatic pilot. She was precise in her explanations about sales tax and part-time help and the value of a good accountant. It was depressing, she thought, to be sensible while her heart was aching.

With any luck this emotional seesaw would level when she finally accepted that David was gone. In the brief time since she'd spoken with him on the phone, she'd slipped through more shadings of mood than a chameleon on a multicolored tablecloth.

"The most important aspect of business," she said, "is to stay in control and to find people you can trust."

"Like David," Beth said. "He was such a good banker. He almost had my financial package all put together."

"Speaking of people you can trust," Jennifer said, ignoring the reference to David, "I've been neglecting my artistic suppliers. It sounds like Clyde has finally stopped playing the piano. I'd better get out there and see what's going on."

As she opened the swinging door into the living room, Jennifer heard the familiar strains of an old, beloved melody. The rich vibration of piano chords trembled through her as she mouthed the words, "You must remember this..."

*Casablanca*, she thought. Rick's Café. David wanting to be noble and brave like Bogey.

"As time goes by."

She glided toward the spinet in a trancelike state. The noises of conversation and clinking ice made a gentle counterpoint to the familiar music. Other faces and forms faded as she gazed at the man playing the instrument. His full lips parted in a gorgeous, dimpled smile, and his smoky-gray eyes shone.

She rested her elbow on the top of the spinet and said the only thing she could say: "Play it, Sam."

"How soon forgotten. The least you could do is get my name right."

"Why aren't you on your way to Malibu Beach?"

"Show biz can wait until morning."

She leaned close to his cute, funny ear and whispered, "Show biz can wait, but I can't."

"How soon can you get rid of this crowd?"

She glanced around the room, locating Beth, who was beaming at the reunited couple like a yenta at a wedding. Jennifer grinned as she motioned to her friend. "Can you play hostess while I escort this future movie executive back to the airport?"

"Only if you promise to give him a thorough send-off." Beth winked at David. "Bon voyage, big fella."

# 3

"THREE SCREWDRIVERS. Maybe four," she admitted as she took a wide misstep off the curb, clutching at her crocheted white shawl. "I don't think I should drive."

David guided her the last few yards to the cab that was double-parked outside her house, but before he could tuck her away inside, Jennifer popped upright and stared into his eyes. "You could drive my van."

"I know," he said, humoring her. "But why don't we take this nice taxicab? He's been waiting for me to come back."

The cabbie leaned out the window. "That's right, pal. And the meter is still running."

David was still trying to convince her that it really was no trouble to take the cab when he heard the chorus from her front porch. "Cal-i-fornia here I come..."

In the instant that he turned and waved to the assembled artists on the porch, Jennifer bounced back to the curb.

"Right back where I started from."

He stepped up behind her, and she half leaned, half toppled against his chest. She snuggled up to him like a soft, furry kitten wanting attention. "Aren't they terrific?" she murmured. "I gripe a lot, but they're really good friends. Even Delilah."

The chorus launched into a rousing version of "She's a Jolly Good Fellow," and Beth, their musical director, paused to dab at her eyes with a handkerchief. The rest of the assemblage harmonized rather nicely except for Philo, who was sipping his drink and glowering.

David couldn't help noticing the hostility emanating from Beth's husband. "What's wrong with him?" he asked.

"Philo? I think he mentioned something about a contract on your life."

"Oh? Any particular reason?"

"He didn't want to see me hurt."

After a cheerful standing ovation from the gang on the porch, Jennifer and David waved goodbye, and he finally got her into the cab. "To the Brown Palace," he told the cabbie. Then he concentrated on Jennifer—funny, sensitive, adorable Jennifer Watt. Despite the wavering eyes and the lopsided grin he thought she was the most beautiful woman he'd ever seen.

Yet he frowned as he watched her. After three tries she finally got her long legs crossed. Another couple of slips and her elbow was resting on her knees. Jennifer wasn't a drinker. Four screwdrivers? Was this his fault?

"Damn," he said. "Maybe Philo is right."

"You think so?" she asked, plucking at the satiny material of her dress. "The red is too obvious?"

"I never wanted to hurt you, Jennifer."

"Well, I like red. Scarlet," she said defensively as her elbow again slipped off her knee. "Scarlett O'Hara."

"It's lovely." With a sigh he resigned himself to the utter futility of a serious discussion. "The dress is lovely."

He couldn't sweep Jennifer off to the Brown Palace Hotel in her condition. It would be too much like taking advantage, and—dammit!—he'd already done that. From the start he'd been deceiving them both, hoping that something could work out but knowing that he had to leave her.

Did he have to leave? He slipped his arm around her shoulders, enjoying the easy intimacy they shared. How could he abandon her when she was so bright, so trusting, so right for him and so...drunk?

As she hummed the refrain from "He's a Jolly Good Fellow" into the sleeve of his navy-blue sport jacket, he leaned forward to tell the cabbie, "Take us to Larimer Square."

"You're running up quite a tab, pal. Hope you own a bank."

David winced at the unintentional irony. Own a bank? At one time that had been his goal. "Not anymore," he said.

The last thing he wanted was the safe, secure life he'd known for so many years. He hated the boundaries and the perks and the neat agendas that defined his existence as a banker.

It was time for David to take his best shot. Until now his course had been well charted. He'd considered every step and executed his plans with the cool detachment of a master chess player. He'd attended the right college and gotten his MBA before it was the fashionable degree. Willingly he'd served his apprenticeship in lower-level management and worked his way up to his very own desk, nameplate, secretary and office. Work, work, work. One achievement topped by another. What a good boy was he!

And he couldn't stand it anymore. When he'd received notification that his crazy uncle had bequeathed him the house in Malibu Beach, something clicked for David. This was the opportunity he'd been waiting for. It was time for him to take a chance.

Quitting his job had been easier than he expected. And he didn't mind subleasing the overpriced condo with options to buy. Or selling the Porsche. He winced. Maybe he did mind parting with his beautiful forest-green sports car, but he knew that all those things had to be jettisoned if he was to have a fresh start and freedom to embark on a new life. He needed the spontaneity and the risk. Until ten days ago he'd had no real regrets.

And then he'd met Jennifer.

The cab pulled up at Larimer Square. David paid the fare, then jostled her into a state of semiwakefulness.

"Now what?" she asked, wrapping her shawl more tightly around her shoulders. "David, it's kind of chilly."

"That's the idea," he said. At the Market he ordered three cappuccinos to go and dragged her across the street. "One for me and two for you," he explained. "We're going for a little ride, Jennifer."

It was one of those clear summer nights in Colorado when the breeze from the mountains curled around old-time streetlamps and the sky seemed very close. City lights bathed renovated Larimer Square in an amber glow.

"But we've just been for a ride," Jennifer objected.

David pointed to an old-fashioned horse and buggy. "Not this kind."

Pure delight shone on her face as she cautiously patted the dapple-gray flanks of the harnessed steed. "Great idea, David. I love it. Do you know I've never done this?"

Obviously, he thought, she didn't comprehend his true motivation. His "great idea" was to keep Jennifer out in the fresh air until her head cleared.

He paid the coachman and helped her into the rear of the buggy. They jolted to a start, heading down the wide beige brick paving of the Sixteenth Street Mall. Jennifer sat bolt upright in the padded leather seat, sipping the cappuccino he had provided and looking around as if she were seeing the skyscrapers of downtown Denver for the very first time.

"Drink your coffee," he coaxed.

"Do you think I'm drunk?" She tossed the comment over at him. "Whacko? Zonked? Loaded?"

"Maybe a little."

"I didn't mean to be. You see, Philo was mixing the drinks, and he put way too much—"

"It's okay, Jennifer."

"I'm feeling a lot better now." Without looking at him she added, "I missed you."

"I'm not gone yet."

"I was practicing."

David caressed the small of her back beneath the shawl. The satiny red material of her unfairly maligned dress felt sleek, as silky as her straight blond hair.

He'd seen her in so many moods over the past ten days. Carefree in the mountains. Astutely diligent over her work. Preoccupied. Happy. Sad. And angry. Despite her constant protestations that she was a single-minded retailer, he adored the free spirit that dwelt within her. She was a complete woman, sometimes unpredictable and always exciting to him.

If only she'd go with him to California, he thought. Could he demand that she accompany him? Hardly. He watched the swaying haunches of the dapple-gray horse pulling their carriage. How would John Wayne handle this situation? David grinned. The Duke would have heaved her over the saddle horn and carried her off, kicking and screaming, into the purple sage.

But he wasn't Duke Wayne, king of Western movies.

His hand rested on the feminine swell of her red-satin hips. His values were more like the lyrics from a Rodgers and Hammerstein musical than a Western movie. David believed in love at first sight, Kismet, violins and candlelight.

"Jennifer? How are you feeling?"

"Bouncy. Buggies aren't much on shock absorbers, huh?"

"I can't believe you'd notice. Not after driving your van."

"No need to insult my van," she bristled. "Just because, once upon a time, you had a Porsche."

"Not anymore."

He didn't have much of anything left. Not much to offer, he reminded himself. Someday he might be an independent producer, an "indy-prod," but right now that was a fancy name for unemployed.

It wasn't the right time to make a commitment, to start a relationship. He could dump his career, his condo and his car—even his car—but David could not rid himself of certain expectations. An old-fashioned morality, he thought, but his standards were deeply ingrained. He believed that a man should take care of his woman, support her and cherish her. He believed that commitment was forever.

Maybe he was more like Duke Wayne than he wished to acknowledge.

Those beliefs were probably the main reason he remained unmarried at age thirty-five. He'd come close a couple of times, but he'd always avoided commitment in favor of his career.

As quaint as it sounded, David wanted to be the breadwinner. Or at least one of the providers. And what if this whole indy-prod scenario blew up in his face?

Once again he reviewed his chances for success as a motion picture producer.

In the plus column: He had a place to live, rent-free. He had considerable savings of his own and the probability of quite a bit more money as a result of inheriting his uncle's house in Malibu Beach, along with its contents. His contacts within the financial world were impeccable. His late uncle's business manager had agreed to meet him. The timing for this career change was excellent.

The risks, however, were huge. Despite a lifetime love of movies and several classes in movie production, he had never actually produced a film. Though he'd read a couple of scripts, he didn't have a specific project under construction. He was taking off from a dead start.

David set his chin at a stubborn angle. He would learn. His training as a businessman gave him an edge, as did his maturity. He wasn't a bright-eyed idealist charging at windmills.

Jennifer must have perceived the tension in his hand, for she turned and gave him a quizzical look before snuggling back in the carriage, comfortably within his embrace. "David," she said in a low, serious voice, "I want to make love tonight."

He gazed at her in disbelief. Had he heard correctly?

"You can lower your eyebrow," she said. "I'm as sure about this as I've ever been about anything."

"I still have to get on a plane in the morning."

"That leaves tonight."

He took her face tenderly in his hands, tilting her chin toward him. Her lovely blue eyes fluttered closed as he joined his lips with hers, tasting the sweet cappuccino cream. God, she was fantastic!

Convulsively he pulled her close. He wanted her, needed her desperately. Her full, curving hips pressed against his hardness and moved with the rhythmic wobble of the carriage.

He could feel her breath in his ear. "Not here, David."

"Right." He settled her back on the leather cushion beside him, keeping his arm around her shoulders. No other woman could penetrate his self-control like that. "Sorry," he said shortly.

"It's okay." She gave him one of those knowing, sidelong glances. "I liked it."

"I loved it," he said.

Did he love her? David exhaled a long breath. Maybe he hadn't put off a committed relationship because he needed to progress further in his career. Maybe he'd just never met the right woman. Until now.

"How are you feeling?" he asked as he opened the second cup of cappuccino and handed it to her.

"Sober as a judge," she said, making a disdainful face at the cup. "Do I need to walk a straight line to convince you? David, I know exactly what I'm doing. And exactly what I want."

He stood in the carriage and spoke to the formally dressed driver. "Take us to the Brown Palace."

The driver tipped his top hat and nodded. "Very good, sir."

"How civilized," David mumbled. "No questions asked."

"What did you expect? Was he supposed to slap you with a glove and challenge you to a duel for my virtue?"

"At the very least there should be pistols at dawn."

"Dawn?" She cuddled up against him. "I was hoping for before dawn."

Inside the ornate, historic Brown Palace Hotel a well-dressed crowd mingled in the lobby. Jennifer leaned close to David and whispered, "Do you think we're formal enough for an illicit assignation at the Brown?"

"A what?"

"I am obviously running with the wrong crowd," she said. "I didn't know so many people in Denver owned sequins and tuxedos."

"Only the best for you, sweetheart," he replied in his Bogart-impersonation voice. "I wouldn't take a classy dame like you to a joint."

She went to buy toothbrushes and toothpaste. "Coffee mouth," she explained with an incongruously sultry wink. "I'll meet you in the lobby in half a minute."

Beneath the glittering chandelier at the front desk David was overtaken by another manifestation of old-fashioned morality. Though the desk clerk was impassive, David stammered as he requested a double room, and he cringed when he said that there would be no luggage. "Just, um, toothbrushes."

## Seems Like Old Times    47

He crossed toward the lobby with the room key hidden in his pocket and tried to shrug off his embarrassment. What had come over him? It wasn't the first time he'd checked into a hotel with a woman who wasn't his wife. But somehow he'd expected this time to be different. He had an idiotic urge to explain to the clerk and the bellman, "This isn't a casual affair, guys. This woman is very, very special."

He spied Jennifer, sitting in a plush brown velvet chair that contrasted beautifully with her bright scarlet dress. She didn't see him, and he paused to admire her sheer loveliness and poise. Her long legs were crossed. Her pose was elegant. She looked utterly at ease in the sophisticated lobby, and David knew that he wasn't the only one who thought so. The white-haired, tuxedoed gentleman sitting next to her was noticing her legs with a polite admiration.

David did a double take. That was no gentleman! That was Bill Waldheim, the chairman of the board of Continental National Bank. David plunged across the lobby.

"So here you are," he announced to Jennifer in a strained voice. He felt like a teenager caught kissing on the porch. "Shall we go to the lounge?"

"I don't think so," she said, gliding to her feet and slipping her arm through his. "You've just spent the last hour sobering me up. Let's go straight to our—"

David pretended to see the bank's chairman for the first time. "Bill Waldheim? What a surprise." Before Jennifer could say anything she might regret later, he made the introductions.

As they shook hands, Waldheim gave Jennifer a distinguished but playful grin. "Charmed. And I do see the resemblance."

David and Jennifer exchanged a confused glance.

"The night watchman's report?" Mr. Waldheim said with a conspiratorial wink. "Ms Lauren Bacall, I presume."

David was aghast. "You read those things?"

"Occasionally they are brought to my attention. And if you weren't leaving us, I would caution you about working late too often. Though I can understand your diligence when you have such an attractive companion. I only wish that Ms Bacall here could convince you to stay at Continental National."

"I'm giving it my best try," Jennifer answered brightly.

"Is our vice president really going to Hollywood?"

"So he says."

"As I mentioned before, Constable, if you ever decide to return to a sensible occupation, we'll have a position waiting for you."

"Thank you, sir," David said.

"Would you two care to join my wife and me?" he asked. "We were just leaving this—the ten thousandth symphony benefit of the summer—for a late dinner at the Ship's Tavern. I know your department had a farewell party for you, but I'd like to give you a proper send-off, too, David."

"Thank you, sir," Jennifer answered before David. "But this is David's last night in town, and..."

"Say no more." Waldheim chuckled as he returned to his chair. "Well, David, I guess I'll see you at the movies."

It wasn't until they were on the elevator that David felt his breathing return to normal. "Of all the people to run into."

"I thought he was cute."

"Cute? Waldheim owns half of the western slope."

The elevator doors parted, and they walked down the hall. David fumbled with the key before he opened the door. As soon as he'd turned on the light, he faced her. "Is this room all right?"

"It's beautiful."

Jennifer sat on the edge of the bed, kicked off her shoes and waited. She watched as he paced around the room. He peeked through the long drapes at the window and peeled off his navy-blue sport jacket before plunking down in one of the plush gold chairs. All the way across the room from her.

He'd bounced back to his feet and was checking out the bathroom when she said, "David? I'm the one who's supposed to be nervous."

"Dammit, Jennifer. I feel guilty about leaving you."

She reclined on the bed, staring up at the dainty little chandelier on the ceiling. The very last thing she wanted to think about was the next morning. Her long legs tightened and relaxed. She stretched her arms over her head and dismissed the future with a deep sigh.

"You were right," he said, "when you told me that I'm not a soldier going off to war. I'm going to a beach house. This is our last night together because of my decision. And now I feel like I've made a mistake."

"I really don't want to think about this."

"Jennifer, I'm going to another galaxy far, far away, and I don't know what's in my future. Developing a career in motion pictures could be a long, painful process. How can I ask you to put up with that? How can I ask you to wait?"

"I'd be lying if I said I was happy that you're moving to Malibu Beach." She sat up and watched him as he continued his pacing. "I'm not. And I don't completely understand your reasons."

"I don't, either," he said, closing the drapes. "That's what makes this so damn hard."

"Would you please sit? I can't carry on a serious discussion with somebody who's acting like a hotel inspector."

He perched on the edge of the dresser and folded his arms across his broad chest. "I don't want to go. I want to stay here with you. But if I don't take this chance, I'll never know what could have been."

"As much as I hate to say it," she admitted, "that makes a weird sort of sense. If you give up this chance, I'll always feel guilty."

"Always?"

"For at least forty-eight hours."

She waited for his smile or his sardonic raised-eyebrow look. Instead, he busily perused the *TV Guide* that had been lying within his reach on the dresser. "Do you believe this? The late-night movie is *Casablanca*."

Glaring with frustration and desire, she sat bolt upright, her fists planted firmly on her hips. "I don't believe any of this. You've lured me up to your hotel room. I'm ready, willing and able to be ravished, and you're reading *TV Guide*."

"Dammit, Jennifer. I'd like to sweep you off your feet. I want to throw you over my shoulder and carry you screaming and kicking away with me. But you deserve better than that."

He crumpled the TV magazine in his hand and hurled it across the room. His voice was low and hard. "I can't promise you tomorrow. I don't have anything to offer you."

"I don't want things, David. I want you. I want to hear you laugh. I want you to hold me." Her voice caught in her throat. "Maybe even to think that I'm the most wonderful woman in the world."

"Don't you know that yet?" His smoky-gray eyes glittered with emotion, and he stood utterly still. "I've never known a woman like you. You're more than wonderful to me."

"Show me."

He crossed the room in two long-legged strides, and she rose to stand inches away from him. "I've been fantasizing about this moment since the first time I saw you."

"And I thought offering an umbrella to a lady in a storm was inspired by pure chivalry."

"Good. Because tonight I'm going to act like a cad."

"David?" She was trembling with readiness. "Please do."

His full lips curled in a smile as his hands slid down her shoulders and lightly grasped her upper arms. Though she'd known that David would be infinitely tender and sensitive to her womanly needs, the actual moment of fulfillment was almost too much to bear. As she gazed into his eyes, she didn't care about tomorrow. Tonight they would make love.

He lowered his mouth to hers, exerting sweet, delicate pressure. His tongue flicked lightly across her lips. There was a slight pause. He pulled away from her again. His gray eyes were questioning.

"Yes, David," she breathed her answer. "I want you."

His apprehensions seemed to vanish with the bright flash of his smile. "You are the most wonderful woman in the world."

He kissed her with a strength and boldness that made a mockery of his prior hesitation. His lips were demanding; his tongue penetrated her mouth.

His strong, powerful arms wrapped around her, and they were locked together in a consuming embrace that betrayed his fierce need for her. Jennifer felt herself being swept into his passion by the force of his need, and she joyfully responded, giving herself fully, completely.

They were fiercely entwined, their bodies clinging, demanding release from the intensity of desire that had been building for ten days. A frenzy churned within her. She wanted him desperately, needed him to fill an emptiness within her that she had not until that moment accepted. He would leave in the morning. There was only tonight, a timeless night.

His demanding tension relaxed, and he separated from her. His fingers fumbled at the buttons on his shirt. "I want to feel you skin against mine, Jennifer. Your softness."

She heard her breath coming in husky gasps as he tore off his shirt, revealing a hard muscled torso. Her first impression of him had been correct; he would make a magnificent artist's model, worthy of the finest sculptor. And yet no artist had the skill to portray the wonder of his living flesh. Marble was too cold. Wood carving was too hard. No substance had yet been discovered that could duplicate the supple strength of his body.

She caressed the V pattern of dark, springy hair on his chest. "David," she said. "I'd like to paint you."

"A little kinky, but I'm game."

When she bent to raise the hem of her dress, he stayed her hand. "Let me."

His hands were hot on her thighs as he slowly eased her dress over the curve of her hips and up to her waist, where the material bunched in a satiny wad.

"Doesn't this thing have a zipper?" he muttered.

"Unfortunately, no. I wasn't planning to be ravished tonight." She held her hands over her head, allowing him to strip off the scarlet dress.

He stared at her slip, bra and panty hose as if they were tremendous barriers to the urgency of his desire.

"I'll take it from here," she said as she quickly wriggled out of her undergarments. "Why is it that they never show this part in the movies?"

While she was occupied with unhooking and slithering, he had removed the rest of his clothing. Magnificently naked, he joined her on the bed.

"Oh, David," she said with a fulfilled sigh. He was marvelously proportioned, the most perfect male she had ever seen. And yet he was totally unself-conscious as his fascinated gaze flowed over her, warming her. His voice was almost reverent as he whispered, "You're lovely, Jenny."

She had never felt more beautiful.

His touch was firm but gentle as he outlined the curve of her waist and the swell of her hips. Still studying her, he cupped her breast and fondled the taut nipple. "I was right," he said. "Your skin is unbelievably smooth. What do they call it? A peaches-and-cream complexion."

"All that means is I sunburn easily."

"Let me taste."

He lowered his mouth to her throat and caressed her flesh. "Delicious," he murmured as he trailed kisses lower until he discovered the fullness of her breast. His tongue teased her nipple to an unbelievable sensitivity.

It was sweet agony, so fine and sharp that she perceived an utter clarity of desire. There was no one, nothing else in the world. She seemed to be floating.

He returned swiftly to her lips, and when their mouths joined and the full length of their bodies touched, a sense of perfect completion burst over her. Jennifer gasped, and his breathing matched her own. His heartbeat hammered above her, synchronizing with her own.

His male hardness throbbed against her, and she separated her thighs, wanting him, needing their flesh to become one flesh. Yet he had not completed her tantalizing arousal.

His deliberate, masterful skill was worthy of the most sensual movie montage. He massaged the nape of her neck, worshiped the juncture of her elbow and wrist, caressed the soles of her feet. When he kissed and fondled the length of her legs—from ankle to calf to thigh—until he discovered the moist center of her desire, Jennifer feared she would explode.

Her body writhed and arched in incredible abandon, needing him, needing the fulfillment he could give her. David waited no longer. He joined himself with her, and his hard thrusts surpassed Jennifer's most exalted imaginings.

She never wanted him to stop. Her hands clawed at his back. Her long legs thrashed against him as he adjusted their positions to provide deeper access.

When the moment of climax came, their release was tremendous. A complete, shuddering tumbling of all the stars in the heavens. She attained cataclysmic satisfaction, uncharted on the scale of emotions.

As she floated back to earth, one thought pierced her perfect happiness. My God, she was going to miss him.

The rest of that long night before the Labor Day weekend would be preserved forever in Jennifer's memories along with the already wilted wildflowers they'd picked in the mountains and the ticket stubs from the Classic Cinema Marathon at the Uptown Theater. So many wishes. So many dreams. How could she count them? How could she save these moments?

This was one time when she was glad that she was a night person with vaguely insomniac tendencies. Hours later, as David slept, her eyes were still wide open, watching him.

As she traced the swirls of dark hair on his chest, he inhaled deeply and exhaled slowly. A smile played across his full lips, but his eyelids stayed closed.

Jennifer smiled back. She wouldn't wake him. Instead, she propped herself up on the pillow and studied him, memorizing his body from his long toes to the thick, sable hair on his head. And every square inch in between.

The passion they had shared was beautiful, and she was glad that he had returned for this one last night. A fitting goodbye.

JENNIFER STOOD AT GATE 22, Concourse B, at Stapleton Airport, wishing that she'd gotten more sleep. Mornings were never her favorite time of day, but this day was absolutely dismal.

She watched as David received his seat assignment in the nonsmoking section. He returned to her side and grinned. "Be a sport, Jennifer. You made me miss *Casablanca* last night. At least give me a farewell scene."

"What did you have in mind?"

"You have one guess."

He took her hand, his thumb playfully tickling her palm. As tired as she was, his minicaresses excited her. She just couldn't get enough of the man. "We can't do what you have in mind," she said. "Not in a public place."

"Wish I had a trench coat," he muttered. "Can't really do Bogart without a trench coat."

"You're not going to make a scene, are you?"

She glanced up at him nervously. The gleam in his eyes told her that he was ready to perform an entire scriptful of scenes.

She shook her head. "What happened to that clumsy, sweet guy who was so embarrassed last night?"

"It wasn't the real me, sweetheart," he lisped, Bogart-style, then launched into a paraphrase of the famous farewell scene from *Casablanca*. "And whatever happens to two little people doesn't amount to a hill of beans in this crazy world of ours. Remember, sweetheart, we'll always have Paris."

Very gently he kissed her.

The boarding instructions were announced, and people began filing out of the waiting area onto the plane. Jennifer felt herself tensing. She didn't want him to leave. It was going to take all her self-control to let him get on that plane and fly out of her life.

She looked into his eyes, imagining that she saw a brief reflection of her own sorrow. But that could not be. If he felt that pain, he wouldn't, he couldn't, leave.

"Will you visit me next weekend?" he asked.

"I don't think so." Though her throat was constricted, she forced herself to continue, "It's better if we don't make plans."

They stood face-to-face, confronting their imminent separation. She stared up at him, hoping against all probability that he would cancel his flight. That he would come to his senses and stay with her.

He traced her cheekbone with his finger. Warm and lingering, his hands caressed her face. His lips brushed her forehead. And then, too soon, it was time for him to leave.

She watched him go, striding briskly toward his uncertain future and leaving her bereft. She should have left the airport right then, forging ahead to her own plans, her own schedules. Already she was late for the craft fair. But she couldn't bring herself to go. She needed to prolong her contact with David, no matter how tenuous.

The waiting lounge was empty except for Jennifer. Standing at the window, she waited for his plane to take off. He could still get off, she wished frantically. He could still change his mind.

When the plane taxied out to the runway, David was still aboard. Now he was really gone. No more hope.

"Unless..."

Before leaving the airport, she purchased an open ticket to Los Angeles.

# 4

JENNIFER HAD never considered herself bashful, not even when she was a child. At one time she had been innocent, even gullible. But never shy. Why, then, had she circled the same block of glamorous Malibu Beach houses four times?

Why hadn't she told David her flight number? She rounded the corner to the beachfront roadway, the street where he lived. Why hadn't she arranged for him to meet her at the airport? Partly because she wasn't sure until the wide-bodied jet was airborne that she would stay on board. And partly because she had wanted to surprise him.

Bad idea, she thought as she parked the compact rental car opposite the beach house that had once belonged to David's uncle. What if he had company? What if he wasn't home? What if he'd decided in the week they'd been separated that he didn't want to see her again?

A thousand dreadful scenarios played in her mind. She'd seen enough old, melodramatic movies to know that the course of true love never did run smooth. He could have been hit by a truck. Or fallen in love with his childhood sweetheart.

She peered at the stone-and-cedarwood house, which was nearly hidden from the street by palm trees and thick, exotic foliage. What would she find inside?

There was only one way to find out. Again she reminded herself that she had never been a toe-shuffling, eyes-cast-downward, bashful child. *Open the door*, she commanded herself.

*No way,* replied this unfamiliar shy person.

She leaned back in the bucket seat and closed her eyes, trying to make sense of her trepidation. David was not a frightening man. He was kind and loving and funny. His touch was as gentle as the salty breezes from the Pacific. He'd called four times on the telephone that week to tell her how much he cared, how much he missed her.

And yet he had the power to hurt her more than anyone else. For her own mental health Jennifer knew that they had to come to terms with this idea of a long-distance love affair. They had to talk about dating other people. They had to take a hard look into the future. Were they lovers or merely good friends?

With her fingertips she massaged her still closed eyelids. *Relax.* She sat quietly. *Just another moment.* She concentrated on releasing the stress between her shoulder blades and the doubts from her mind. There was a great deal to be nervous about. So much was unspoken and so much at stake. If he slammed the door on their inconvenient relationship, Jennifer feared she would shrivel up into a lonely old hag.

Instead, she heard a door being opened—the car door on the passenger side. Before she could react, she felt strong, unforgettable arms pulling her into a sideways embrace. She opened her eyes and saw David's perfect, roguish smile.

"I thought I'd better come out here," he said, "before you ran out of gas."

"I wasn't sure about the address. These streets are all so curvy and..." She stopped herself. Her excuses sounded feeble even to her. "How did you know I was coming?"

"The Great Davidini knows all and sees all," he said, placing his divining hand to his forehead. "I see a craft shop in Denver. I see a woman behind the counter—"

"Okay, swami."

"The woman was Beth," he said in his normal voice. "I called the shop, and she told me you were on your way and your flight number, but it was too late to make it to the airport. Why didn't you let me know you were coming?"

"I was feeling shy. Unsure of myself, unsure of us. David, we're going to have to talk this weekend, and make some decisions."

"Absolutely." As he took her face in his hands and kissed her, she felt her nervous constriction begin to release. The knot in her stomach loosened. But it didn't go completely away. There was a taut residue of tension that would not disappear.

"We will talk," he promised. "But first I have something really exciting to show you." He slid out of the car and dashed around to her door to open it. "Luggage in the trunk?"

She nodded and blindly handed over the keys. Those doubts would be settled. She couldn't spend another week of sleepless nights and distracted days. And yet, in his presence, her questions seemed unimportant. They were together again. Nothing else mattered.

Before she'd set her sandals on pavement, he'd opened the trunk and grabbed her small canvas suitcase.

"I'm amazed," he said, giving her an appraising once-over. "That is the most modern outfit I've ever seen you wear."

She smoothed the cotton folds of her short, perky, peach-colored culotte dress. "When in Malibu, do as the Maliboians."

"Maliboians?" He hooked his arm through hers and whisked her across the street.

"Maliboites? That can't be right. It sounds like a gum disease. What do they call people who live here?"

"Rich." He hustled her along the sidewalk to his front door.

"You look modern yourself," she said, noting the smooth fit of his pale blue knit shirt and white tennis shorts. Under her breath she added, "And not at all like a banker."

He wasn't listening. David was so enthused that he was practically babbling. "You couldn't have timed your arrival better, Jennifer. I have just made an earthshaking discovery. Well, maybe not earthshaking. But really exciting. Damn, I'm glad you're here."

He ushered her inside, and Jennifer had to pause for a moment to catch her breath. The natural stone foyer created a suitable medieval setting for a full-sized suit of armor and crossed swords. To her left was a sprawling sunken living room furnished in blue and beige with another rugged stone wall and a fireplace worthy of Xanadu's opulence. She looked back at the armor. "Who's this?"

"My uncle was an evil jouster in 'The Black Shield of Falsworthy.' Remember that gem?" He set her suitcase down and urged her up a wide iron staircase that hugged another natural stone wall. "Come on, up here."

Jennifer touched the stone for balance and was surprised to feel a glowing warmth. "David? Why is this rock hot?"

"Passive solar system. My uncle might have been a recluse, but he was no dummy." He anxiously beckoned her the rest of the way up the stairs. "I'll show you the whole circulation with the pumps and the storage panels and everything. Later."

At the top of the stairs Jennifer was surprised to discover a spacious office area. The house didn't seem that large from the street, possibly because it was dwarfed by the relative size of some other Malibu Beach mansions.

The desk faced a huge picture window with a spectacular view of the Pacific shoreline. Overhead, a bank of skylights offered terrific natural lighting. Jennifer smiled her approval. "This would make a dynamite art studio."

"Sure, sure." David yanked her toward a door at the northern end of the room. "We'll talk about it—later."

In his haste he almost shoved her inside the darkened room. Taking her by the shoulders, he directed her to a chamois-colored leather sofa. "Sit."

"David, what are you doing? What's so important?"

"Jennifer, Jennifer, Jennifer, please sit down."

With a final confused glance she plopped herself on the sofa. Before joining her, David went to the wall that stretched before them and flicked a switch. The wood paneling slid back, revealing a forty-two-inch-square television screen.

He did a fair impression of a mad scientist's cackle before taking his place beside her on the sofa and aiming a remote control device at the screen.

Jennifer heard a loud buzzing noise. The screen was lit with the black-and-white image of a muscular superhero in gleaming cape, dark tights and a medieval-looking doublet. His headpiece sparkled, vaguely resembling the pointed stinger of a hornet.

Background music swelled, and Jennifer recognized the five-tone trumpet blast from David's teasing description. A deep voice intoned, "Wasp Man. He flies. He soars on silver wing. Men of evil, beware his sting."

"Your Uncle Clayton?"

"Who else?"

On the large screen Clayton Forbes moved with athletic grace into the takeoff position. His cape billowed out like wings, and he soared as the deep voice continued, "Many years ago Dr. Mike Michaels, hardworking scientist, was accidentally caught in the blast of a zenium-croton explosion. He escaped without injury. His fiancée, Dr. Susan Swan, was not so fortunate."

The screen showed the well-built Forbes dressed in explosion-torn clothing of the fifties. He gently lifted a woman in his arms. His face was streaked with tears.

"I don't believe it," Jennifer remarked. "A superhero with sensitivity. Does Alan Alda know about this?"

The announcer continued, "Shortly thereafter, Mike discovered his unusual powers born of the zenium-croton proton particles. He defied gravity. He had the strength of a hundred men. He could see for twenty miles. He was...Wasp Man. As Wasp Man, he vowed never to speak until evil was forever silent."

The beginning of the episode showed a huge, sterile-looking laboratory. Clayton Forbes—also known as Mike Michaels, also known as Wasp Man—was hunched over a microscope. A woman, dressed in what Jennifer thought was a terrific nipped-waist suit, stumbled across the lab and fainted at Mike's feet.

"That's Harriet Kelton," Jennifer said. "My God, I never thought she did anything like this."

David used the remote control to freeze the scene. "More important, Jennifer. This is a lost episode. When I was growing up, I saw every single one of the *Wasp Man* shows. Some of them I saw three and four times. This wasn't among them."

"And?" She waited for the punch line.

"My uncle saved all the lost episodes."

"I didn't realize you could record those old television shows."

"They were on kinescope. I found the original reels in a vault in the basement." He tossed the remote control on the sofa and went to open the curtains. "Uncle Clayton was always big on gadgets. He probably had the kinescopes reproduced as videotapes as soon as the technology was available."

He went to the wall beside the television screen and pointed to a glassed-in, floor-to-ceiling case full of videotapes. "Sixty

Seems Like Old Times 63

six episodes of *Wasp Man*. *The Black Shield of Falsworthy*. *The Viking*. *The Silver Rose*. *Dark Moon on the River*. They're all here. Every movie my uncle appeared in is here."

"Can we watch *The Silver Rose*? I loved Harriet Kelton in that." Jennifer gave a nostalgic sigh. "I cried and cried...."

"Don't you realize what this is?"

"A nifty videotape collection?"

"This," he said with an extravagant sweep of his hand, "this is my future."

Oh, yes, she remembered, the future. That was what she had come to Malibu Beach to discuss. Their future. "What do old movies have to do with our future?"

"I'll be rich!" He rubbed his hands together and cackled like a cinematic mad scientist. "Rich, do you hear me, rich."

"Yes, David?"

He calmed his voice to its usual tone. "Here's my thought. My uncle left me this house and all its contents. If these tapes can be rereleased into network or cable syndication, I might be able to collect residuals. Anyway, I put a call to my uncle's attorney, and he's going to check the possibilities."

His enthusiasm both amused and disappointed Jennifer. Though she wished him the best of luck in his new career, her blatantly self-centered hope was that David's dedication to movie-making would be wearing thin. It would be so much easier, she thought, if he'd decided to return to the peacefully stable world of banking.

He looked to her for encouragement. "What do you think?"

"I'm sorry, David. I didn't follow all that."

"Pay attention, Jennifer. I'm talking about us."

"Us?"

"Me and thee, sweetheart. If I can syndicate *Wasp Man* and become impossibly wealthy, you can move out here permanently."

"What?" Where had that come from?

"I've missed you." He went down on one knee before her in the classic gesture of an old-fashioned proposal. Taking her hands in his, he cleared his throat. "I want you to live with me."

"Live with you? Here?"

"'Tis humble," he said grandly. "But I call it home."

"I can't move out here. I have responsibilities in Denver. Remember? Watt's Up?"

"Sell it. Start over here."

"I can't do that," she objected. She retrieved her fingers from his grasp. "And you know I can't. You're familiar with my loan package at the bank. I've barely recouped my start-up costs. After Christmas I might move into the black instead of the red."

"Be a sport, Jennifer. I'll front you the money for a new store out here."

"It's more than the money," she said firmly. "I'm very pleased with all I've accomplished in Watt's Up. I love my store. And I love my house. And I love Denver. I don't intend to give it all up."

His gray eyes sparkled, compelling her attention. "I want you with me, Jennifer. Not just on weekends, but always."

"That's not fair, David." She stiffened, fighting off the seductive power of his gaze. "I want to be with you, too."

"So? What's the problem?"

"I've finally proved to myself that I can be responsible. I can't just up and quit."

"Even if I was wealthy beyond your fondest imaginings?" Still kneeling before her, he playfully slid his hands along the outside of her thighs. "Move in with me?"

"Why don't you come back to Denver and live with me?"

"Doesn't work that way. I want to be your man, Jennifer. I want to take care of you."

"No, David." She slapped at his questing fingertips.

"Is that so bad?"

"It's not bad or wrong," she said. "It's just not what I want right now."

"Okay." He stood, marched off a couple of paces and took a seat on the sofa beside her. "The syndication thing is a long shot, anyway. I'm sure the production company owns all the rights."

Side by side they sat, staring at the unmoving shadows on the huge television screen. It seemed to Jennifer that their relationship was just as frozen as the image of Clayton Forbes and Harriet Kelton. She wouldn't budge. Nor would he.

He stretched his long, bare legs straight out in front of him, drooped his head onto his chest and sighed. "How come this never happens to John Wayne?"

"What are you talking about?"

"The Duke." He unfolded to a standing posture again and took a few bowlegged cowboy strides. His voice lapsed into a John Wayne drawl. "Now, listen up, pilgrim. We're going to do things my way from now on."

"Fat chance, Duke."

"I'll tell ya I'm sorry—" he continued his drawl "—and then I want to kiss ya and kiss ya and kiss ya until you can't get kissed no more."

She couldn't help laughing. "That's worse than your Bogart impression."

"You think that's bad? You've never heard my Cagney."

"David!" she said loudly before he could go into yet another impersonation. "Sit."

He sat. "Yes, ma'am?"

"What is with you? You've been bouncing around this room like a yo-yo. Up and down. Back and forth. It's making me tired to watch you."

David leaned back against the sofa and stared up at the acoustical tile ceiling. With a whoosh of a sigh he tried to shake off the tension he felt building inside. Her arrival had affected him more than he'd expected. Before she arrived, he'd known that he missed her. Seeing her here was different. It made him realize how empty the house had been without her, how empty his life had been.

His farfetched scheme about syndicating the *Wasp Man* episodes, including the "missing" shows, had not seemed so important before she came. Now it was vital. It meant overnight success. He would have something to offer her.

"David?" She called him back from the world of Hollywood dreams.

"I'm sorry, Jennifer."

"You don't have to apologize. Just explain. Why are you so hyperactive?"

"I guess this is what grasping at straws looks like."

"I have a better idea." She took his hand and placed it on her waist. "Grasp me."

He didn't need another invitation. His arms encircled her in a sweet, comforting embrace.

Her body felt so good against him. During the week apart he'd imagined the feel of her ten times a day. As he nuzzled the slender column of her neck, he realized that the reality was more wonderful than any fantasy. He pulled her to him, reveling in the fragrance of her perfume. The sensation of holding her quenched his jitters and lit a very different sort of excitement within him. "God, I've missed you."

As he pulled her inexorably toward him, his knee touched the remote control for the giant television screen. And the *Wasp Man* episode blared.

"Dr. Michaels, you must help us." Harriet Kelton's voice trembled fearfully.

Startled, Jennifer jerked away from David and stared at the television as Clayton Forbes, in a reassuring baritone said, "I'll do whatever I can, ma'am."

Grumbling, David reached for the control, but Jennifer stayed his hand. "Your uncle isn't bad," she said. "He's got a terrific voice."

"I can't believe this." David slumped back on the sofa. "I'm being upstaged by my deceased uncle."

"It's the family resemblance that I find intriguing," she said. "You really do look a lot like him."

"I thought I looked like Clark Gable."

"Both."

Jennifer grinned as Harriet Kelton emoted. "She's terrific, isn't she?"

"You're really a fan, aren't you?"

Jennifer bobbed her head as she watched Clayton Forbes usher the sobbing Miss Kelton from his lab.

"Next time I'm in Denver," he promised, "we'll go up to the mountains and meet the real live Miss Harriet Kelton."

"Could we? Really?" She turned to him with a real glow of excitement. "When are you coming to Denver?"

"Sometime. Of course, if you lived out here, you could hobnob with lots of stars. Jane Fonda? Sissy Spacek?"

"Not interested. My favorites are Harriet Kelton, Katharine Hepburn and Lauren Bacall. None of whom live in Lotusland."

A trumpet blast from the television signaled that Wasp Man was going into action. Jennifer compared the muscular physique on the screen to David's, running her hand speculatively along his lightly tanned leg. "Do you look as good as your uncle in tights?"

"Tights? I never gave them much thought."

"You might be cute," she teased, tiptoeing her fingers across his thigh. "I've got some panty hose in my luggage."

From the desk in the other room they heard the telephone ring. Gratefully David went to answer. "Saved by the bell."

Jennifer continued to watch *Wasp Man*. Clayton Forbes, she decided, had charisma. Or sex appeal. Despite the trite plot and inane dialogue, there was something fascinating about the man.

Perhaps that same charisma had been inherited by his nephew. Any other man who dared to zap her with the "my career is more important than yours" philosophy would have been picking himself up off the floor. Surely he hadn't meant it. Not the chauvinistic way it sounded. Or had he?

She concentrated on the television screen where Wasp Man single-handedly demolished three seedy-looking thugs. That was how she wanted to handle her questions about their relationship. Like Wasp Man. She visualized the questions as if they were punching bag balloons.

Where will we live? Pow!

Whose career comes first? Biff!

What kind of commitment is this, anyway? Ka-blooey!

She heard David return to the room and turned to him. "This show isn't half bad," she said.

"It isn't half mine, either." Like the dissolve to black at the end of a movie, his former enthusiasm had faded. He aimed the remote control and flicked off the television as Wasp Man shook Harriet's hand and flew off into the wild blue yonder.

"That was the lawyer on the telephone. My uncle didn't own syndication rights to *Wasp Man*. In fact, his possession of these tapes was something akin to video piracy, and the lawyer advised me to return the kinescopes to the company that produced the series. He did, however, say that the company might be interested in a *Wasp Man* revival."

"Which means?"

"If I want to promote *Wasp Man* and arrange for a sale to cable or network, they'll be happy to take the profits."

She followed him through the office and down the stairs. "So? You're not going to be rich and famous overnight?"

"Don't gloat, Jennifer."

"I'm not gloating. Look, David, I won't pretend that I'm thrilled about your career. But I wish you well."

He led her through a gleaming, modern kitchen. "How about a walk on the beach? If I can't convince you to move out here because I'm going to be a mogul, maybe the natural beauty of the Pacific will change your mind."

He opened sliding glass doors that led to a cedar deck, and they went outside. Though the skies were hazy, the view of the rolling white breakers crashing along the sandy shore was fantastic. Jennifer stood at the edge of the deck and inhaled the briny air.

"What do you think?" he asked glumly. "Nothing like this in dear old Denver."

"You don't have to give me reasons." She turned her back on the view and confronted him. "Believe me, David. I want something to work out between us as much as you do. And your idea of opening a Watt's Up in Malibu Beach isn't totally impossible. But it has to be my decision. Like your new career was your decision."

"My career?" Though he laughed, David couldn't disguise his sarcastic disdain. "Career is a bit pretentious to describe what I've got going."

"Rome wasn't built in a day."

"True, but Atlanta burned in about an hour and a half, courtesy of David O. Selznick. *Gone With the Wind*, 1939. Everything moves fast out here except success."

"Give yourself some time, David. And give our relationship time, too. We're both adults. We'll figure something out."

They descended the stairs to the beach. There were surfers and swimmers and sunbathers, but the beach area was not crowded. Jennifer and David took off their shoes and strolled near the high-water mark.

*Sand between my toes,* Jennifer thought. The golden warmth and the lullaby of the surf offered enticing, sensual arguments for packing up and moving to California. Snow would soon be falling in Denver. Though the Colorado climate was mainly sunny and pleasantly arid, the southern California coast was unbeatable for sheer hedonistic pleasure. "Slow down, David."

"You're not into power walking?"

"There's a new way of walking?" she questioned. "Of course. I should have known. This is trendy southern Cal."

"What about an old-fashioned game of Frisbee?" Like a bored tour guide, he pointed out the distant bikini-clad figures leaping and chasing swirling discs at the water's edge. "Or a jog along the beach?"

"David, my idea of heavy exercise is getting up in the morning." To emphasize her point she slowed her pace further. "Guess I'm not a California gal."

"I'm beginning to think I'm not a Hollywood kind of guy, either."

At his words she glanced up quickly. Was he considering an end to his budding career?

Her quizzical gaze was not returned. He pulled a pair of dark Ray-Ban sunglasses from his shirt pocket and hid behind them.

Even without the sunglasses he looked guarded, she thought. Preoccupied. And kind of sad. Damn. She kicked at the sand. His slowed-down gait reminded her of a funeral march. Though she wanted David back in Denver, it had to be his willing decision. Not the result of failure in Malibu Beach.

Jennifer knew the frustration in her own dreams deterred. Trying to cheer him up, she launched a new topic. "Tell me about your Uncle Clayton. Where did he go after the *Wasp Man* series ended?"

"Nowhere. There was an accident on the set. In one of the fight scenes my uncle took a sharp blow to the throat. His vocal cords were damaged. He regained his voice, but it was husky, more like a whisper."

"Really? He couldn't perform?"

"I don't know." David shrugged. "There might have been operations or vocal-training methods. My mom came out here to encourage him, but he refused to do anything. They had a fight—a big fight. That was when my summer visits ended."

"Why?"

"A combination of things." He kicked a stone. "I had Little League and summer camp. Needless to say, Mom wasn't thrilled about me spending time with her weird brother. And he didn't make any special efforts to invite me."

"Does that make you sad?"

"A little," he admitted. "I didn't know Uncle Clayton all that well, but I remember that he was always exciting and fun. I'd listen to him practice his lines at night. During the day I'd hang around the set. Or play with his incredible gadgets. We'd broil hamburgers on the grill. And there were parties."

From his wistful tone Jennifer could easily imagine six-year-old David peeping around the banister to spy on his celebrity uncle's wild parties. "This is beginning to sound a bit like hero worship. Did you want to be Clayton Forbes when you grew up?"

"Sometimes." He pushed his sunglasses back into place on the bridge of his nose. "When you're a kid, it's pretty spectacular to have a movie star for an uncle."

As they strolled beneath the warm but overcast skies of Malibu Beach, Jennifer refrained from further questions, and David appreciated her silence. It would have been easy for her to draw conclusions about his boyhood admiration.

What a cornball scenario: Boy comes to Hollywood to follow in famous uncle's footsteps. Falls on butt.

Of course, David had given serious thought to the possible connections. Living in his uncle's house, he couldn't avoid the memories and the associations. And he had deduced that he wouldn't be in Hollywood if it hadn't been for Clayton Forbes. Not only had Forbes encouraged David's interest in movies, he had also shown him that it was possible to achieve success in that highly competitive field.

Was he trying to be like his uncle? To relive Clayton Forbes's life? No. David had his own identity. He wasn't an actor. He didn't want to be a star...except for maybe in Jennifer's eyes.

"Is there any more to the story?" he heard her ask. "After the accident did your uncle give up everything?"

"I'm not so sure he did," David said thoughtfully.

"But he retired, didn't he?"

"He never made another film. But that doesn't mean he became a recluse. That was my mother's version of the story, and she was real angry. She said that he'd told her his injury was retribution for abusing his talent."

"By playing the part of a silver-winged superhero?"

David nodded. "Even though he started in silent films, Uncle Clayton was a respected Shakespearean actor, trained in England at the Old Vic."

"But that doesn't make sense," she said. "If he was so repulsed by *Wasp Man*, why did he save all the tapes?"

"Good question." David stopped in his tracks. He took off the sunglasses and stared at her. "Jennifer, my love, you're absolutely right. Keep talking."

"About what?"

"I'm not sure. Whatever comes into your head."

"Well, it seems to me that your uncle had a fascinating career. Theater, silent film, movies and television."

"Yes." He nodded. "Go on."

She could almost see him making connections in his mind. Connections to what? "I don't know what else to say."

"How about this? Most of his career is on tape in that screening room. Even a couple of Shakespearean performances."

"The life and times of Clayton Forbes," she said.

Since they'd reached a secluded portion of beach, David's whoop of excitement startled only Jennifer and a couple of wading gulls. She recovered quickly. "I beg your pardon?"

"Want me to do it again?"

"Please don't. There may be off-shore whales trying to sleep."

He placed his hands on her shoulders, holding her at arm's length. "Jennifer Watt, you're the most brilliant female since Madame Curie, the best detective since Miss Marple—"

"I agree," she interrupted. "What caused you to notice?"

"You've given me the best idea of all time." He dropped his hands to her waist. "The best."

"Uh-huh." Her eyes narrowed skeptically. "Want to tell me all about it?"

"I'll produce a documentary about Clayton Forbes. His life story."

His energy revved up, and she could feel the excitement flowing through his fingertips. She'd never seen anyone so convinced about a creative project. Whether or not the life of Forbes was a classic, it was the movie that David needed to make. "I love it," she said.

He leaned close to her, directing her gaze to a nonexistent marquee. "Clayton Forbes, consummate actor."

They were cheek to cheek when he turned to her, surrounding her in his embrace. "He flies," David whispered. "He soars on silver wing."

Jennifer slipped her arms around him. For the first time since she arrived, she felt as if they were together. Meeting his silvery gaze, she asked, "What will you call it?"

"*Foibles of Forbes?*" He kissed her lightly on the tip of her nose and drew away to study her. "*Clayton's Calling?* Have I told you that you're beautiful?"

"So are you." She grinned and went up on tiptoe to kiss his chin. "*The Call of the Wasp?*"

Without warning he dipped her in a low, dramatic embrace. "What about *The Sting*?"

"It's been done." She tilted back her head, seeing an upside-down cyclorama of clouds and sand and sea. And in the midst of it all was David, finally looking happy and strong and terribly sexy.

"I've got it," he said. "The title!"

"Yes, David?" she breathed.

He kissed her thoroughly. "*Wasp Man Speaks!*"

# 5

WASP MAN HAD SPOKEN. And the earth had moved.

The next morning Jennifer stretched luxuriously beneath the cream-colored satin sheets and folded her hands behind her head. Though the warmth of morning sunlight touched her closed eyelids, she wasn't ready to be awake. She wanted to spend the entire morning—until maybe noon—remembering the night before.

Words were inadequate to describe David's lovemaking. She replayed visual images and recalled sensations that had tingled through her. Jennifer felt completely satisfied.

A fresh and fragrant whisper tickled across her cheek. She twitched her nose and opened her eyes. *David.*

He trailed the white rosebud across her lips. "Good morning, sweetheart," he lisped like Bogart.

She gazed up at a huge skylight above the bed and grinned. "Last night there were stars," she said.

"And not all of them were in the sky," he added. "Is madam ready for her breakfast?"

He eased her into a sitting position. From beside the bed he produced a wicker bed table containing coffee, poached eggs and a buttered croissant. With a flourish he dropped the white rosebud into a silver vase.

"There's something you ought to know about me," she murmured, averting her gaze from the eggs. "I'm not a morning person."

"I'll keep it in mind." His electrifying smile was already operating at full wattage as he leaned close and brushed her cheek with a kiss.

"So that means..." Her words trailed off as she gazed up at him and smiled with sweet semiconsciousness. "How come you're all dressed?"

"Remember? *Wasp Man Speaks?* We have a ten o'clock meeting with my uncle's attorney."

She glanced at the clock beside the bed. It was only nine, plenty of time.

"To be there on time," he said, "I have to leave in five minutes."

Far away in the recesses of her unawake mind, a distant alarm pinged. "Fine," she said with a lazy yawn.

Her internal alarm pinged louder. "Five minutes?"

He grinned at her and nodded.

"Five minutes!" she cried. "I've got to get up. I've got to get dressed. Why didn't you wake me earlier?"

"I didn't have the heart to disturb you, Jenny, my love. You looked so peaceful."

"But I wanted to go with you."

She struggled to climb out of the bed without overturning the wicker tray. When she was halfway free of the satin sheets, she realized she was stark naked.

After a full night of lovemaking there was no point in being modest. Still, she felt a little silly. He was wearing his business suit. She was wearing her birthday suit. "Don't worry." She clutched the sheets in a clumsy toga. "I can be ready in four minutes."

He held out a terry-cloth robe, which she grabbed and slipped into, hurriedly fastening the sash as she charged toward the bathroom. At the door she pivoted. "Whose robe is this?"

He guided her into the bathroom and opened the louvered doors of a linen closet to reveal a neatly folded stack of similar robes. "Ladies' sizes—small, medium and large. Apparently Uncle Clayton wasn't such a recluse after all."

"Good old Wasp Man?"

"And there's a drawerful of skimpy black bikinis. Those appear to be one-size-fits-all."

"How about that Uncle Clayton?"

"Could I make a suggestion, Jennifer?"

She turned the faucets in the combination bath and shower, starting a gush of water in the tub. "How do you make this a shower?"

She fiddled with a spigot on the wall, flipping it clockwise. The water became an overhead spray—a sudden spray. Jennifer was drenched. She stood upright, faced David and groaned. "You had a suggestion?"

He took a towel from the heated rack and placed it gently around her shoulders. "You stay here. Slip into one of those one-size-fits-all bikinis. And catch some rays on the beach. I'll be back in time for a late lunch."

"Well, I'm sorry to miss your meeting, but it's a deal."

She wound the towel around her head and tried to look awake as she held out her hand. "Shake?"

With a smooth, easy movement he grasped her hand and yanked her into his arms. The shock of his surprise embrace changed to pleasure as she gazed up into his gray eyes. She sighed and relaxed, comfortably resting her cheek against his chest.

Wet hair and all, she could have gone back to sleep on the spot. She nuzzled against him, breathing in the fresh laundered scent of his cotton shirt.

"I've got to go, Jennifer."

She listened to the words rumbling and vibrating in his chest. "Sounds wonderful."

Though his embrace was loose and lazy, his kiss revealed a tenderness and sensuality. The heat of his soothing caresses penetrated the terry-cloth fabric on her back and inspired an excitement within her. Impossible. She trembled with newly alert desire. *Oh, my, it's much too early*, she thought.

His tongue slipped between her lips. Slowly and delicately he explored the inside of her mouth. She glided into his mood, rubbing herself against him like a damp, sleepy cat stretching in the sunlight.

She never imagined passion could be like that. Easy and comforting—it was an altogether pleasant way to awaken.

"I have to go," he said.

She hummed a soft assent.

And then he really kissed her. Squeezing her against him, ravishing her mouth and starting up all sorts of passionate, aroused cravings. It was quick but thorough.

When he released her, Jennifer was limp.

He straightened his collar, winked and said, "Here's looking at you, kid."

David sauntered out the door.

Jennifer, breathing hard, massaged her wet hair. "I wonder if he'd want to start off every day like that."

BY THE TIME DAVID RETURNED, Jennifer had dressed, eaten breakfast and found a comfortable chair on the deck. As she sipped her third cup of coffee, she flipped through a magazine. Her wider attention was focused on the magnificent, every-changing panorama of the Pacific coast.

She loved the familiarity of his light kiss on her cheek as he joined her on the deck.

"How was your meeting?" she asked.

"Perfect. The company that owns syndication rights to 'Wasp Man has agreed to give me free access to all tapes. They

## Seems Like Old Times 79

consider my proposed documentary film to be excellent publicity for possible resyndication of the series."

She applauded.

"And how did you enjoy your morning?"

"Very relaxing."

For a moment she sat quietly, beaming at him. "You look so happy, David."

"I am. For the first time I feel like I made the right decision."

"Moving out here?" Her own pleasure crumpled a bit.

"Getting involved in filmmaking," he corrected. "And having you here, on my side, has made the difference."

"You know, David, one of the reasons I came out here this weekend was so that we could have a serious discussion."

"Seriously?"

"Don't tease. We've got a lot to talk about."

"Such as?"

"Well, for one thing, I don't like people making decisions for me. Like when you say, 'Move your shop to Malibu Beach.' Or 'I decided to let you sleep in.'"

"I understand."

"You do?"

"Sure," he said. "How long will it take you to pack?"

"That's exactly what I mean," she said, exasperated. "Did you ask me? No. Did you consider my plans? No."

He was grinning mischievously like the Cheshire cat in *Alice's Adventures in Wonderland*. It was difficult, she thought, to stay irritated with somebody who was so obviously pleased with himself. "So," she said, "where did you want to go?"

"May I ask you now?"

"Yes."

"Are you sure?"

"Yes, David."

"Would you like to meet Harriet Kelton?"

"Back near Denver?"

"Yes, Jennifer. That hasn't changed in the past five minutes. She still lives in the mountains west of Denver."

She bounded out of the deck chair. "Five minutes," she shouted. "It will take me five minutes to pack."

JENNIFER WAS WILLING to postpone her serious discussion for an opportunity to meet Harriet Kelton. She was also willing to throw her things into her suitcase, race to the airport and catch the next flight back to Denver.

"I can't believe it," she said as they disembarked from the taxi in front of her house. "I'm going to meet Harriet Kelton."

As they jostled along Highway 285 toward Conifer in her aged Chevy van, David attempted to explain why he thought a meeting with Harriet Kelton was imperative. "Though the company that owns the rights to *Wasp Man* has indicated that they will cooperate, there are a lot of other film clips I'd like to use. Before I go to the trouble and expense of obtaining those rights, I want to be sure about a couple of things. Harriet Kelton knew my uncle well. I think she'll be able to give me some answers."

He glanced over at Jennifer. Though she drove with cool skill, there was something wild about her. Her usually straight, neat hair whipped in the breeze from the van's open windows, and her wide blue eyes glittered.

"Jennifer? Have you head a word I've been saying?"

"Is Miss Kelton expecting us?"

"We're not going to a royal audience, Jennifer. I've met the woman before. She's an average, sweet, little old lady."

"I doubt that, David. The woman was a star. She's been kissed on the lips by Cary Grant."

"Silly me." He rolled his eyes. "I didn't realize that a kiss from Cary Grant qualified a woman for immortality."

Jennifer quivered. "There'll never be another Cary Grant. I once stood on the street for two hours waiting to catch a glimpse of him walking into the Carousel Ball."

"You're acting like a groupie, Jennifer."

"I just can't believe it." She chuckled to herself. "She was nominated for an Academy Award, wasn't she?"

"Twice. But I wouldn't mention that if I were you. She's a bit touchy about Janet Gaynor winning the first Academy Award for Best Actress."

As Jennifer hummed "There's No Business Like Show Business," David concentrated on the notes he'd been making. Creating a business proposal was no problem for someone with David's experience in business loans. He was dealing now, however, with film.

He mentally reviewed the information from the several classes and American Film Institute workshops he'd taken in film production and management. He would need a writer to give continuity to the documentary and a film editor to put the pieces together and a cinematographer to film new interviews. The market needed to be pinpointed. Distribution had to be arranged. A complete financial package had to be compiled before he actually started production.

First, he needed to verify his impression that Clayton Forbes was worthy of documentation. He needed information from the source—people like Harriet Kelton who could tell him that Uncle Clayton was an outstanding example of an actor who participated in theater, silent film, talkies and television.

For his own satisfaction, David wanted to reinforce his newfound understanding of his uncle's retirement. There was one apparent contradiction that worried him. If his uncle had been happy and content during the years following his accident, why hadn't he been involved in any other films?

He glanced up from his notes. "Turn north at the next exit."

"I was thinking," she said. "Has Harriet Kelton turned into a fruitcake, like Gloria Swanson in *Sunset Boulevard*?"

"That was a fictional character."

"It was chilling," she said with a shudder. "I'll never forget Norma Desmond, the formerly glamorous movie star, surrounded with memorabilia from her career, pretending that her glory had never faded, that she'd never grown old."

David felt his own presentiment of nervousness. Was that why Uncle Clayton surrounded himself with videotapes of his career? Because he was unable to shake the past? It was a grotesque fantasy, one that was more suited to the version of Clayton Forbes his family propagated.

Strange, he thought. His mother had always told him that her brother was weird, but the attorney considered Uncle Clayton to be a smart businessman and a witty golf companion. All those bikinis in the bottom drawer attested that his uncle wasn't such a recluse after all.

Jennifer parked in the blacktop lot, and they peered through the windshield at a large three-story, whitewashed frame building. Though the bright blue shutters did not blend in with the natural forested surroundings, tall spruce trees clustered protectively around the mountain dwelling. A discreet sign proclaimed The Lodge.

"It looks like a movie set," Jennifer exclaimed. "Like one of those old-time hotels in Western movies."

"It is picturesque."

"How many people live here?"

"Ten or twelve people live in the main building itself. Plus there are several small cabins scattered about on the grounds. And a barn with stables. Most of the lower floor of this building is a social area—parlor, game room and dining room."

"I still can't believe I'm going to meet Harriet Kelton," Jennifer said.

"Believe," he advised as he climbed out of the van. He came around to the driver's side and held open her door. "Everybody who lives here was involved in theater or film, and they can be an exciting and excitable bunch."

"All retired?"

"They're over sixty-five," he explained. "Of course, this isn't a medical facility. Nobody here is seriously ill."

"How old is Harriet Kelton?"

"Mid-seventies, at least."

As Jennifer followed the flagstone walkway leading to the veranda, she experienced a thrill of anticipation.

Her sensation had nothing to do with the actual appearance of The Lodge. It was charming and placid in the afternoon sunlight. The lawn was well kept. Colorful geraniums nodded from flower boxes at the windowsills, and chokecherry shrubs formed a thick hedge at the boundary of the yard.

As they mounted the wide concrete steps to the veranda, Jennifer noticed a flurry of movement in her peripheral vision.

"Hold it," a scratchy voice shouted.

Startled, Jennifer turned to face him.

"Smile, honey." A flashbulb exploded, and the puckish little man crowed with delight.

"Hope you don't mind." He grasped Jennifer's hand and pumped hard. "Has anyone ever told you that you look like Lauren Bacall?"

"Not recently." She exchanged an amused glance with David. "I'm Jennifer Watt. And we're here to see Harriet Kelton."

"Guess who I am." He tore the Polaroid picture from the camera while he obligingly posed facing them and in profile. "Do you recognize me?"

"I'm sorry," Jennifer said hesitantly.

"Of course you don't." He triumphantly thumped his chest. "They call me Charlie Peyton, King of the Extras. Never been a star, but I've been in more movies than anybody. I've bumped shoulders with Alan Ladd, held a machine gun on Jimmy Cagney and died a rebel in *Gone With the Wind*. Now I just keep things running at this place."

Jennifer grinned and glanced up at David. Excitable? That description was an understatement for the manner of this leprechaun who bounded up the steps beside them while continuing his cheery monologue. "If I'd learned how to ride a horse, I could have been in fifty more pictures."

"How are you doing, Charlie?" David asked.

"David, my boy." A mask of sadness slipped over Charlie's ebullience. "Sorry about your uncle."

"Thank you, Charlie."

Having fulfilled his duty to the heir, Charlie turned back to Jennifer. "Clayton Forbes and me were good friends. I designed that fancy-do house of his in Malibu Beach."

"With the solar heating system?" Jennifer asked.

"Just one of my inventions." He opened the front door and ushered them inside. "Take a seat in the parlor. I'll tell Miss Kelton you're here," he called over his shoulder as he dashed up the staircase. They stood at the entrance to a large, sunlit room with a fireplace, a piano and several conversation areas. The furnishings were attractive but inconsistent. One area contained heavy wingback chairs and ornate tables. Another had modern director's chairs and chrome lamps. Still another was early American. Jennifer's gaze darted from one area to another. It was as if several interior decorators had conspired in one room and failed to reach an agreement.

"This room gives a whole new meaning to the word *eccentric*," she said, studying an old-time sepia photograph arrayed beside a splashy modern oil painting. "And I absolutely love it."

"Told you so."

A tall, gaunt man unfolded from a large wingback chair. Before he strode across the room to meet them, he straightened the perfect crease in his trousers, checked the one inch of white cuff extending from his suit jacket and adjusted his regimental striped necktie. "Good afternoon," he said in a thick British accent. "Would you join me for a cup of tea?"

"How kind of you to ask," Jennifer replied, allowing herself to be drawn to the Victorian corner of the room.

With elegant grace he laid one finger on his cheek and studied her. "You are an extremely beautiful creature, but not an actress. You play the piano. However—shame on you—you don't practice often."

"That's true," she said.

"You are an artist," he said with a dramatic flourish. "One of your specialties is watercolor portraiture. Your home—rather Victorian, I would suppose—is in Denver where you own a retail art shop."

Jennifer gaped. "How did you know all that?"

"Elementary, my dear." He settled back in his wingback chair and proceeded to light his meerschaum pipe.

In the blink of an eye Jennifer recognized him. How could she not? "You played Sherlock Holmes," she said. "In dozens of movies."

"Only four," he corrected. "Mr. Basil Rathbone then claimed the part for his own. But I rather enjoyed Holmes."

"And he especially enjoys this guessing game," David said. "Jennifer Watt, this is Lionel Wolff. I gave him your biography over the phone when I called to ask Harriet if we could visit."

"But he didn't do you justice," Lionel said. "By the by, my offer of tea was real."

A plump, bustling woman whisked into the room with a full tea service on a squeaky-wheeled cart. With speedy aplomb she dodged around throw rugs, chairs and tables as she brought the cart to a halt beside Lionel. "Here you go, lordship." With only a brief pause for breath she patted David on the shoulder. "So sorry to hear about your uncle. Clayton Forbes was a real honey of a guy. A prince."

She swiveled around to face Jennifer and winked. "Besides, he had a great body."

She exited.

"That was Gloria," David said. "I have never seen the woman light in one place for more than three seconds."

Before Lionel could ask whether Jennifer preferred one lump or two, they were joined by three more women, each clad in a jogging suit of a different color—magenta, yellow and turquoise.

The introductions took quite a long time since each actress—none of whom Jennifer recognized—included a brief summary of her film credits along with her name. Jennifer was elected to pour the tea, and the afternoon snack took on a party atmosphere.

Gloria returned with a tray full of croissants and cookies. She announced over the conversation, "Listen up, everybody. This young man, David, is going to make a film about Clayton Forbes."

"Wait!" David waved his hands. "It's not final."

She continued over his objection like a steamroller. "And I think we should all pitch in and help. The kid is new at this. And there's over two hundred years of experience right here in this room."

"Two hundred years?" drawled the woman in magenta. "Speak for yourself, darling."

"Do you have a script?" asked the woman in turquoise. With a dramatic sweep she pushed her very red hair off her forehead. "I'm not a screenwriter, but I have been working on my memoirs."

There was a loud groan from the others.

"Actually," David said, "it wouldn't be a film. My idea right now is sort of a documentary biography using lots of clips from my uncle's performances. I wanted to use his career to show the variety and growth of American cinema. However, I welcome all of your input and advice. I'm here to get information."

There was no trumpet fanfare, no drumroll, no introduction, but Jennifer was aware of another presence in the room. She turned her head to watch as Harriet Kelton made her entrance. She was small, delicate-looking and yet bristling with energy. Her silvery-white hair had been coiled into a smooth chignon.

Jennifer swallowed the lump in her throat. The ethereal beauty of the young Harriet Kelton had not been lost, only transformed. Her radiant star quality transcended age, and Jennifer was not disappointed.

The woman in the yellow jogging suit turned toward the entryway and rolled her eyes. "H–e–e–e–re's Harriet!"

After one glance at Harriet, magenta suit sucked in her stomach and muttered, "How does she do it? The wretched woman never diets, and she never gains a ounce."

"It's because she's a vampire," turquoise muttered. "Fresh blood must be low in calories."

Despite the catty comments, Jennifer noted that their expressions were friendly. Interesting. Were they covering up feelings of resentment? Their greetings were sisterly and affectionate, and Jennifer decided that the snide remarks must have been habitual rather than malicious.

Then she heard Lionel, speaking for her ears only. "Remember, Jennifer. Things are not always as they seem. All of them are accomplished actresses."

A warning? Were these three the witches from *Macbeth*, updated to jogging suits? Before she could respond to Lionel, David made the formal introduction. "Miss Harriet Kelton, this is Jennifer Watt."

"And how did you meet this special friend?" she asked. Her head-to-toe survey was an unabashed appraisal, and Jennifer wished she'd taken the time to apply fresh makeup and run a comb through her hair.

"In a rainstorm," David said. "After a movie."

"One of mine?" Harriet asked in a sweet, melodious voice.

David shook his head. "I regret that it wasn't."

"No matter," she said in disappointed tones that told Jennifer it mattered a great deal. "I grant my approval, anyway."

As the petite lady extended her hand, Jennifer wondered whether she should genuflect or kiss the pearl and diamond ring on Harriet Kelton's pinky. When she grasped Harriet's hand, the flesh was warm and firm. And the older woman's gaze had, indeed, indicated a pleasant acceptance.

"I don't mean to be standoffish," Harriet said. "Though I was married four times, I never had children of my own. I must exercise my grandmotherly prerogatives on the families of my dear, old friends. And Clayton was a very, very dear friend."

"I understand," Jennifer said, even though she wasn't sure that she did comprehend all the nuances of meaning. Had Harriet and Clayton been lovers? David had mentioned that possibility. Jennifer decided that she didn't want to know for sure. She had a sense about Harriet Kelton—to admire her from afar would be far more satisfying than discovering tiny feet of clay.

As they settled back down to a congenial tea, Jennifer observed with interest. She had been around actors before, but these people were seasoned professionals. The most insignificant pleasantry took on dramatic overtones. The woman in the magenta jogging suit imbued every comment with tragic overtones. The yellow jogger nearly wept when she spilled crumbs on her ample breast. Lionel's voice had lowered to an incredible resonance.

They were vying for the spotlight, Jennifer realized, performing without a script. She looked over at David, who seemed either unconcerned or unaware of the highly charged emotional undercurrent.

Charlie Peyton burst into the room. Obviously, Jennifer thought, the man was incapable of anything so mundane as an average walk. He was carrying a stack of photo albums. "I heard you were doing a documentary," he said. "And have I got a deal for you."

He flipped open the top photo album, putting it on David's lap, and pointed. "There's me with your uncle."

He handed an album to Jennifer. "Go on, take a look at these. Photography has always been my hobby. And these ain't Polaroids."

He dashed out of the room, flinging a parting comment over his skinny shoulder. "I got something else that's going to knock your socks off."

As they oohed and aahed over the pictures—alternately flipping through the pages to find themselves and reminiscing about others—Jennifer turned an artistic judgment on Charlie's photographic skills. Not bad. The black-and-white photos showed a real talent for framing and capturing moments.

She lingered over a picture of Clark Gable, chatting with a woman in a wide hoop skirt. He was dressed as Rhett Butler and the aura of gallantry and romance fairly oozed off the page.

Jennifer glanced over at David, comparing his features with Gable. Simultaneously he met her gaze. His smoky-gray eyes were warm, communicating an affection that could never be posed or planned. She was glad, incredibly glad, that he wasn't an actor. Relationships were complex enough without having to decipher meanings within meanings.

She looked at Gable, then back at David. There was a definite similarity in their features—mainly in the full, roguish smile. The difference was that, for Jennifer, Gable would always be a distant, two-dimensional image on a screen, a suave hero who suggested strong sensuality. David Constable, on the other hand, could deliver.

Jennifer snapped back to reality when she heard the discordant blast of five trumpet notes. Gloria announced, "Wasp Man. He flies. He soars on silver wing. Men of evil, beware his sting."

Charlie Peyton, dressed in full Wasp Man regalia, leaped through the entryway. He spread the silver cape and buzzed around them.

David was on his feet, applauding. "Where did you get the outfit?"

Charlie struck a pose. Though the navy-blue tights bagged around his knees and his puffed-up chest didn't fill the tunic, Charlie Peyton looked heroic. "I used to do some of the stunts in the show. This was an extra outfit."

"It doesn't begin to fit," sniped the woman in the magenta jogging suit.

Gloria scurried around Charlie. "It could. With a tuck here and a dart there."

"It's perfect," David said. "If I do the film, may I use the costume?"

"No problemo, kiddo."

"Great." He offered his arm to Harriet, who gracefully accepted. "Please excuse us for a moment."

He waited beside the sofa at the far end of the room until she'd made herself comfortable. Then David sat beside her. "Harriet, may I ask a few personal questions?"

"Certainly, dear. I do, however, reserve the right to abstain from reply. And I never tell my age."

"After my Uncle Clayton's accident, what happened?"

"My dear David, may I be frank?"

David cringed inside but kept his expression noncommittal. "Actually, I'd prefer that."

"Clayton was a vital, energetic man. Very talented but occasionally lacking in discipline. He chose to retire because he no longer wished to exercise his craft. I know for a fact that he received film offers after the accident."

"What about his voice? Was it possible for him to perform?"

"Indeed, it was. He was not stricken dumb." She bristled. "You must excuse me, David. I was rather annoyed with Clayton. You see, one of the films he refused would have included a very plum role for an actress not unlike myself."

"I see." He cleared his throat, knowing that if he didn't drag Harriet back to the topic of Uncle Clayton, they would be discussing her career. "Harriet, I would also prefer frankness."

She bobbed her head once in assent.

"Was my uncle crazy? Did he have a nervous breakdown?"

"Whatever gave you that idea?" She laughed in silvery, tinkling tones. "I didn't always approve of Clayton, but he was utterly sane."

"Not a recluse?"

"He merely retired more emphatically than most people—removing his telephones and referring all his mail through a secretary. And he did a great deal of traveling."

"He did? I wasn't aware of that."

"There is a great deal you don't know, David."

"You're right. And that's why I need your help. I'd like to make up for the film role Uncle Clayton caused you to lose. Harriet, would you narrate the documentary?"

"My dear boy—" she paused coyly, then winked "—I would be honored."

David gazed across the room. Everything was working so smoothly. Pure serendipity, he thought as he caught Jennifer's eye. He winked and gave her a thumbs-up sign.

She winked back and returned her attention to a very long, involved joke that Lionel was telling. *Thumbs-up. He's going to do it. David's going to make a movie.*

Despite her reservations about his new career and her doubts about the stability of their relationship, she had caught his enthusiasm and excitement.

Maybe Beth had been right when she'd said that David was her destiny. Maybe Jennifer should stop worrying about the form of the relationship. Lie back and enjoy, she thought. No matter what crazy thing he did, David Constable seemed destined to be her real-life hero.

# 6

DURING THE NEXT TWO WEEKS Jennifer revised her opinion of David more times than Wasp Man battled the nefarious forces of injustice. At times he was "her hero"—a dedicated, fledgling producer, valiantly creating a video documentary about Clayton Forbes. Other times he was the very model of a preoccupied workaholic.

Sometimes he was the perfect attentive lover. But not often enough. Too frequently he was gone—shuttling back and forth to Hollywood, clearing up legal and financial details related to the production.

All the time, every day, Jennifer was aware that her relationship with David had changed her life. The peace and quiet she'd taken for granted had become a precious commodity. And she still hadn't found the opportunity for that serious discussion. Though the boundaries of their relationship remained as much in flux as flotsam and jetsam, there were days, hours and minutes when she was happier than she'd ever been before.

Times like today, however, were incredibly difficult.

It was a rainy Thursday afternoon and Jennifer hadn't expected much customer traffic in her shop. She'd been ready for a quiet time—a perfect occasion to dust the stained-glass windows or rearrange the silver and turquoise Navajo jewelry in the locked display cases.

Instead, Watt's Up was the site of an impending battle. Jennifer paced the hardwood floor of her shop, adjusted a pen-and-ink drawing of a windmill and wished that David would materialize whenever and wherever he was needed like Wasp Man. *He flies. He soars on silver wing.* His plane was due over an hour ago, but he still hadn't arrived for the meeting.

Her jaw clenched. She didn't want to get involved in this altercation; that was David's job. Besides, both of these women were dear to her in different ways. Harriet Kelton was her idol. And Beth Andrews had been her best friend for years.

Worse yet, Jennifer admitted to herself, this fight was partially her fault. When David was pondering his choices for crew to work on the documentary, Jennifer had cheerfully piped up, "What about Philo and Beth?"

"Philo?" David had given her a dubious look. "Well, he does have a good reputation as a cameraman."

"And he does editing, too," she urged. "I know Philo isn't Mr. Sunshine, but he is very talented. And he would love to be involved in something artistic."

"Maybe," he'd said reluctantly. "What about Beth's qualifications?"

"She's a writer, a poet."

"A scriptwriter?"

"She's done scripts for commercials and videos. And we both know that she's going to need extra income if she decides to go ahead with her print shop."

After more discussion David had agreed to both of her suggestions. Actually, he had been much more willing to hire Beth, whose credentials were less solid than her husband's. "Because," David had said, "Beth will be easy to work with."

Jennifer glanced across the counter in her shop at the two women. Thus far Beth had been easy to work with. But Jennifer suspected that her friend had just reached the end of cooperativeness. Beth's lips were pressed together in a thin, tight line, and she was fidgeting uncharacteristically.

"David should be here soon," she said. "Right, Jennifer?"

"Real soon," Jennifer replied wishfully.

"I simply do not understand," Harriet Kelton intoned. "Why not begin with a montage of my film clips?"

"Because," Beth explained, "this is supposed to be the story of Clayton Forbes."

"But I am the narrator. It shan't hurt to show my qualifications."

"It just doesn't work, Miss Kelton."

Jennifer heard the slight tremble in Beth's voice. Her sentimental friend was no match for the strong-willed determination of the former star. Harriet Kelton was accustomed to getting her own way. She hadn't risen to the glamorous heights of Hollywood success by being reasonable.

"Dear child," Harriet said, pressing her advantage. "When you have been in the business as long as I, you develop a sense of what's best. We will start with my montage."

"No." Beth stamped her foot. "I've rewritten this opening ten times already. Not again. Not unless David tells me to."

"It's a writer's duty to please the star."

"You are not the star."

Jennifer could stand no more. She braced herself on the counter. "Time out!" she loudly interrupted.

Red-faced and tense, Beth fell quiet. Harriet stared disdainfully. "Jennifer, dear? Is there a reason for you to be involved in this discussion?"

"For one thing, this happens to be my shop."

"Quite true, but we aren't disturbing any of these quaint little knickknacks."

"Knickknacks?" Jennifer snapped. Her blue eyes darkened as she beheld an intricate mosaic of stained glass, a graceful pottery chalice and a handwoven Indian blanket. Knickknacks? In a controlled voice she said, "There is absolutely no point to discussing the script until David arrives."

"Of course, you are right," Harriet said, dipping into her endless wellspring of charm. "Unfortunately, I cannot wait for long. Charlie Peyton drove me into town, and I wish to return before nightfall."

Beth growled, "It's no use, Jennifer. She's going to bitch whether David is here or not."

"If you don't mind," Jennifer growled back, "I'll mediate."

Harriet offered a spritely smile as she picked up a whittled wooden blue jay. "This is adorable, Jennifer. Would you feel appeased if I made a purchase?"

"Is that supposed to be a bribe?"

"Consider it a payment for the use of your facility." Her acid inference contrasted with her innocent tone. "You must try to understand, Jennifer. Beth and I are the talent."

*And what am I?* Jennifer thought. *Chopped liver?*

"We are not attacking each other personally," Harriet explained breezily. "We are creating."

"I see," Jennifer said, her rear molars grinding. "And you wouldn't expect a humble shopkeeper to understand."

"Heavens, Jennifer. I meant no insult."

"Oh, no?" Beth leaped to her friend's defense. "That's exactly what you meant. I've had it with your ego, Miss Kelton. I'm leaving before I say something I really regret."

Beth turned up her collar and stomped out the door into the rain.

Harriet gave a little tsk-tsk. "Poets can be so touchy."

The door never closed, and the bells hanging above it tinkled cheerfully as Charlie Peyton bounded inside, Polaroid camera in hand. He crossed to Jennifer and spread several damp photos on the counter. "Here's what you've got on this street," he said. "Toy store. Bookstore. Boutique. Another boutique. Coffee shop. Restaurant. Kitchen stuff. What's missing?"

"Live ammunition," Jennifer said, glaring at Harriet.

"Movie memorabilia," Charlie announced. "You could put a section right over in the corner. Heck, Jennifer, with all my stuff and my contacts, we could have a real going concern."

When the door swung open again, the bells crashed instead of tinkling. Philo Andrews strode directly to Jennifer. The man looked as if he were about to explode, but he kept his voice low. Low and hard. "My wife is out in the car, sobbing her heart out. I don't expect this Kelton fossil to understand, but I want you to know, Jennifer, that I consider this David's fault."

"Fossil?" Charlie blurted out. "Who are you calling a fossil?"

"A reference to me," Harriet said serenely. "I understand that fossils are quite valuable these days."

"Out!" Jennifer shouted. "All of you. Out."

"I have an appointment," Harriet said.

"Go to the café next door, and I'll tell David where you are."

Jennifer spun away from them and took sanctuary in the back room of her shop. Though a whirlwind of tension spiraled through her, she forced herself to be still, leaning her forehead against the cool, white wall until she heard the thud of footfalls as they trooped out the door. The pealing of the silver bells hanging above the door was followed by blessed quiet.

She sank into a plastic chair beside her cluttered desk. Her head throbbed. Her eyes ached. Damn. Everything seemed to be out of control.

Her best friend was sobbing in the car. Philo blamed David. Harriet Kelton, her idol, was miffed. And Charlie was pushing her to open a movie memorabilia store. Actually, she thought with a brief return to normalcy, Charlie's idea was not a bad one. But how could she dream of adding more responsibility to her already burgeoning load?

She heard the bells, announcing someone else in the store. With her luck it was probably a thief.

She rose to her feet, but before she could make another move, strong arms wrapped around her. A deep masculine voice tickled her ear. "Where have you been keeping yourself, sweetheart?"

"One step away from the funny farm." She leaned against his chest and snuggled in his arms. "I missed you, David."

"Me, too."

"We seem to be saying that a lot lately."

"It's going to get better," he reassured her.

"I hope so." She wriggled out of his embrace. "You'd better run along. Dear Harriet is waiting next door. By the way, did she ever play the role of Lucretia Borgia? Vampira?"

"Okay, Jennifer. What's wrong?"

"How would I know?" She paced away from him and took a seat behind her desk. "I'm not the talent. How could a humble shopkeeper like me have an opinion?"

David circled her desk in swift strides. He twirled her around in her swivel chair and stared into her eyes. "Your opinions are the only ones that count. I'm not telling you that because you're beautiful and I adore you. It's the truth. You, Jennifer, are the most perceptive, intuitive person I've ever known, and I value that quality." He gently kissed her forehead. "Now why are you so upset?"

There were a million things she wanted to tell him, ranging from the tiny irritation of chipping her favorite coffee mug to the major stress of him staging meetings in her shop. She wished that they could have a month for debriefing, the leisure to chat about unimportant things.

Instead, she heard the door to her shop jingle open—again. The noise of talking, walking and laughing indicated that a

## Seems Like Old Times

horde had entered. "Jennifer?" Beth called. "Jennifer, come on out."

David gave her shoulders a squeeze. They'd had two minutes to communicate. Not long enough, Jennifer silently protested as she followed David to the front counter.

When Jennifer saw Philo with Beth on one arm and Harriet on the other, she wondered if she'd fallen into "The Twilight Zone." All three of them were smiling happily as they welcomed David.

"We have no more problems," Philo announced. "Harriet has agreed to follow Beth's script."

"That's right," said Harriet as she clung adoringly to Philo's arm. "If there's one thing I've learned in my years in the cinema, it is this: Make friends with the cameraman."

"Then it's settled?" David asked.

As The Three Musketeers made assenting noises, Jennifer concentrated on Harriet. That valuable fossil was up to something. It must have taken considerable charm to conquer Philo's temper. Jennifer wondered why Harriet had bothered to make that effort.

"Terrific," David said. "You'll be happy to know that I have the final financing in place, and the distribution arrangements are almost set."

"Who's distributing?" Philo demanded.

"It looks like the Public Broadcasting Service stations are interested. I pitched *Wasp Man Speaks* as a pilot project, the first of several programs focusing on the development of American cinema and television."

"National exposure." Philo's gratification shone through his thick veneer of cynicism. "I've waited a long time for this."

"However," David warned, "I'm not going to be able to pay more than minimum."

"He'd do it for free," Beth said, hugging her husband.

"Oh, no," he immediately protested. "That's the one thing that separates the pro from the amateur. I get paid for it."

To Jennifer, Philo's attitude sounded a great deal like the world's oldest profession, but she wasn't about to discourage this newfound camaraderie. "Of course, Philo needs to be paid," she teased. "How else will he pay for beard grooming?"

"I'd like to begin shooting tomorrow," David added. He looked to Harriet for approval. "At the retired actors' home near Conifer?"

"Everyone there will be delighted," Harriet said sweetly. "And now I would like to make a small suggestion."

They all waited, expecting a problem.

"I wish to invite you all—" she paused dramatically, giving each person a warm glance "—to dinner this evening. It shall be my treat."

"I'm sorry," David quickly countered. "Jennifer and I have plans."

"Of course you do," Harriet said quickly. "How thoughtless of me. You two young lovers need to spend a bit of time together."

"More than a bit," David said, taking Jennifer's hand.

Harriet beamed. "You make an adorable couple."

THE SECOND HAND on the clock in Watt's Up moved with leaden ticks, and Jennifer watched it impatiently. Twelve more minutes and it would be six o'clock. She could close the store.

Her dinner date with David wasn't until eight, but she wanted to take a long soak in a hot bath. It had been a long, trying day, and the problems with Harriet and Beth hadn't helped any. Nine minutes until closing.

She cringed as the bells above the door tinkled and two customers strolled into the shop. "May I help you?" she asked, trying to sound encouraging rather than impatient.

"Just looking."

*Great*, Jennifer thought. *Just looking.*

No matter how impolite or detrimental to good will, she planned to hustle these "just looking" people out the door at the stroke of six o'clock.

Five minutes until closing. The telephone rang.

She pounced upon it. "Watt's Up. May I help you?"

"Perhaps," a whispering voice replied. "Try. Try to remember."

"This is a terrible connection." Jennifer jiggled the telephone receiver, trying to rid it of the crackling static on the line. "I can barely hear you."

"Then you must listen to the voice within yourself. Allow those who have gone to rest quietly. Life is for the living."

"What? What are you talking about?"

"You must tell David. Speak to him, to…"

The last words were garbled and indistinct, but Jennifer thought the whispery voice was repeating that she must speak to David. About what? Loudly she demanded, "Is this some kind of joke? Who is this?"

"Don't be afraid," the voice whispered. "I am a friend."

The receiver went dead.

"Some friend," Jennifer said. As she slammed down the telephone, she noticed the two customers staring warily in her direction. "Wrong number," she explained.

The customers were edging toward the door, and Jennifer made no effort to stop them. It was closing time, and neither customer nor weird phone call nor dark of night would stay her in her rush to leave the shop.

She locked the door behind her customers and flipped the We Are Open sign to Closed—Come Again.

She thought nothing more of the strange phone call until she and David were bounding along in her van on the way to Alexander the Greek's restaurant. David was driving, and Jennifer leaned back against the Leatherette upholstery to watch the play of streetlights on his handsome profile. "Do you remember that Doris Day movie?" she asked. *"Midnight Lace?"*

He nodded. "It was a thriller, wasn't it? And the woman kept getting these bizarre telephone calls."

"You've never done that, have you?"

"Made a bizarre phone call? Not intentionally." He pulled up at a stoplight, turned to her and grinned. "I've been tempted to give you an obscene call, but I wouldn't know what to say."

"I doubt that."

"Really. I don't go to porn movies."

"Never?" she teased.

"Stag parties in college, but I don't remember much. You know me, Jennifer. Beneath this Brooks Brothers suit beats the heart of a proper, conservative, stodgy old banker."

"Yeah," she agreed. "A sweet, old-fashioned guy."

"Why do you ask?"

"Right before closing I had an odd call. The line was full of static, and the voice did this husky whisper. Whoever it was seemed to want me to tell you something."

"Me? What?"

"I'm not really sure," Jennifer said. "Something about memories, and life is for the living. But the voice wasn't threatening. It sounded a little sad."

"This might be carrying sensitivity a bit far," he said. "You don't have to be understanding to telephone perverts."

"It wasn't obscene."

"What was it, then? Did you recognize him?"

"I don't know that it was a him. It was a husky whisper." She tried to imitate the voice. "Be sure to tell David."

"Tell David what?"

"I'm not sure. Life is for the living?" She gazed through the windshield. "David, where are we going? Alexander's is north from here, not south."

"I need to pick up some special lights for tomorrow."

She slumped down in the seat. Another intrusion into their limited time together. This was not an auspicious beginning to a romantic evening.

"Jennifer, this phone call worries me. I don't know why anyone would give me a strange message through you, but I sure as hell don't like it."

"I wish you'd told me about this stop on the way to the restaurant."

"It'll only take ten minutes, Jennifer. Then the van is loaded and ready to go." He paused, glancing toward her. "We *are* using your van to go up to Conifer, aren't we?"

"Yes," she said shortly.

"I'm sorry, Jen. Everything is so hectic that I forget half the things I need to do. It might help if I wasn't living out of a suitcase in my good buddy Tom's extra bedroom."

She felt a twinge of guilt. They had briefly discussed the possibility of David's moving in with Jennifer and rejected it. "You never should have subleased your condo," she said.

"Well, I didn't know I was destined to become Denver's cut-rate version of Cecil B. deMille." He parked in a lot outside a photographer's studio. "Want to come in?"

"I'll wait here."

Though he gave her hand a pat before he leaped out of the van, Jennifer sensed his irritation. That was his problem, she told herself.

And she was irked with this unscheduled stop. Her problem.

Carefully she folded her hands on her lap. Her outfit that night was a vintage sleeveless shirtwaist dress in pale pink that she had combined with a fashionable peplum jacket. Jennifer had taken time and trouble with her appearance: coordinating the shade of her lipstick, selecting the right shoes and styling her hair in a softly curling version of her usual straight pageboy. David hadn't even noticed. And whose problem was that?

She knew there was a delicate balance to be maintained in any relationship. How much to give? How much to take? Though her natural impulse was to try with all her might to please him, that system too often led to resentment. She and David were mature adults. Certainly they could work out the details of their relationship. If only they had more time together...

The side door of the van rumbled open, and David carefully placed several lights inside. He slammed the van door and rushed back to the driver's seat. "Voilà!" he said, starting up the engine. "Only seven minutes' delay in our schedule."

She reached across the space between their separate seats and touched his arm. "Someday, David, we are going to have to set aside an entire day for talking."

"I would like to schedule a day that would last for the rest of our lives."

"That's very poetic, David. But not practical."

"I can be practical with the rest of the world." He caught her hand and raised it to his lips. "You look wonderful tonight."

"I thought you'd never notice." She ran her fingers along the lapel of his navy-blue suit. "You're looking good yourself."

"You like these banker suits, don't you?"

She winked. "It's only because I haven't seen you in your Wasp Man tights."

It wasn't until they were seated at Alexander the Greek's and sipping white wine from tulip-shaped glasses that Jennifer eased back into the topic of their relationship. "If you could have anything different about me, what would it be?"

"I wouldn't change a hair." He drained his wineglass and poured more from the bottle the waiter had left on the table. Though it was a Thursday, the restaurant was pleasantly crowded. "I suppose turnabout is fair play. What would you change about me?"

"You first," she insisted.

"Okay. Promise not to get mad?"

"Absolutely."

"I'd want you to be more patient," he said. "Right now it's important for me to focus twenty-four hours a day on the documentary. Some days I feel like I'm running in ten different directions at once."

"I know the feeling."

"This isn't going to last forever, Jennifer. Bear with me until it's over. Then our relationship will take the priority it deserves. Time for us won't always be sandwiched between meetings and connecting flights."

She twirled her wineglass and smiled across the table at him. "I guess I can hang in there, David. And I'll try to be more supportive."

"Hey, you've done a lot already. It was your contact with Beth and Philo that got me a writer and a cameraman."

"Don't let Philo hear you say that. He thinks he's a cinematographer."

"Maybe he is," David allowed. "I can't figure out that guy."

She leaned back in her chair, enjoying the dimly lit, ethnic atmosphere of Alexander the Greek's. A drummer and a bouzouki player took a casual stance on the edge of the dance floor and began playing softly. Their lilting rhythm suited her mood. The lighting, wall hangings and displays of earthen pottery gave the restaurant an intimate, crimson glow.

"What happens next?" she asked. "Is it like *Zorba the Greek*? Are we going to break plates on the floor?"

"No plate breaking, but there is a belly dancer," he said. "In case you've conveniently forgotten, what happens next is you tell me what you'd like changed about me."

"Two things. I want you to share your emotions with me. Not just when you're happy. I want to know when you're sad or angry with me."

"I'm never angry with you."

She rolled her eyes. "That's not possible."

"What's thing number two?"

"The reverse of what you are saying. I want all your time. I'd like to dominate your every thought." Teasing, she batted her eyelashes. "All Jennifer. Twenty-four hours a day."

"You'd be surprised how close I am to that state. I might not always show it—part of my old-fashioned reserve—but I'm insane about you."

"Insane?"

"Absolutely. I'm being fitted for a straitjacket tomorrow."

The very idea of David being insane about anything was so absurd that she giggled. Despite his roguish smile and his glamorous choice of occupation, he was still as stable as a banker. *My banker. With interest.* He was right when he said that she liked to see him in his utterly conservative three-piece suits. "You'd probably look good," she said.

He raised one eyebrow. "Am I missing something here?"

"You'd look good in a straitjacket," she explained.

"Of course it depends on the tailoring."

"Absolutely," she said with mock seriousness. "Fit and fabric are so important in straitjackets for the well-dressed man. I think you'd look best in gray pinstripes to match your eyes."

He stretched his hand across the table, and she slipped her fingers within his grasp. "I've missed this," he said. "We haven't had much chance to just be together."

"To be silly together?"

"To be anything. I like this, Jennifer. A lot."

"Know what I think?" She gave his hand a little squeeze. "You'd look even better out of your straightjacket."

As they were serenaded by the sensual drumbeat and the melody from the lute-shaped bouzouki, Jennifer's gaze met his across the table. His eyes gleamed in the soft pinkish light. He seemed to be laughing, teasing and promising at the same time.

She concentrated on the promise. Tonight when they made love, she knew it would be special. She had to grin. They were always incredible together. He never failed to ignite her passion.

"It's times like these," he said, "that I wish we both smoked."

"Why?"

"Think movies, Jennifer."

"Do I have to?"

"Remember all those smoldering scenes where the hero reaches across the table, fondles the heroine's hand and lights her cigarette? And the one where he lights both cigarettes in his mouth and hands one to her?"

"Obviously," she said, "that was before the surgeon general's report."

"It was still suggestive."

"David," she said with a vampish wink. "I think we're beyond suggestions."

The increased volume of the music precluded further conversation, and they settled back to watch as Aziza the belly dancer rippled her way across the dance floor in the center of the restaurant. She was a big, voluptuous woman, and her dancing was more athletic than sensual.

Jennifer and David scooted their ringside seats together for a better view. The temperature seemed to rise several degrees as the crowd joined in, clapping along with the music and weaving to the sensuous bouzouki tempo.

"I'd love to dance like that," Jennifer shouted to David.

"Go for it. There's a lot of space on that floor."

"I'd be too embarrassed."

At a signal from Aziza, the audience called out in unison, "Hey!"

Aziza drifted into the audience, randomly selecting a partner to dance along with her. As partner number one found his own belly dance rhythm and sashayed back to his place, Aziza turned her heavy-lidded gaze upon David.

"Hey!"

Aziza beckoned. David protested, but Jennifer encouraged. "Here's your chance, David. Loosen up. Get rid of some of that old-fashioned stiffness."

"Stiffness?" He rose to the challenge. "I'll show you who's stiff."

In a fluid, dramatic movement he stripped off his suit jacket and clapped his hands above his head as he went toward Aziza the belly dancer.

"Hey!"

Jennifer was delighted with his performance. David was energetic, and he had a natural charisma, the legacy of Clayton Forbes. He attempted to follow Aziza's sinuous moves but gave up almost immediately. Instead, he dropped to the floor and did push-ups in time to the music. Then he bounced back to his feet and swung through a series of toe touches before getting into the thrumming bouzouki beat with vigorous hand clapping.

Jennifer laughed delightedly. She could forgive any klutziness when he met her gaze and smiled his dazzling smile.

"Hey!"

When Aziza moved on to another man, David approached Jennifer. He held out his hand to her. She demurred for only an instant before stepping out onto the dance floor. The music seemed to be twanging within her as she shimmied and swung her slender hips with glorious abandon.

Jennifer waved her arms, seductively appealing to David with graceful gestures and laughing and stamping her feet. The rhythm switched to a slower, gently pinging tempo.

"Hey!"

David grasped her firmly around the waist and lifted one hand above his head. She imitated his pose. Gracefully they circled each other in an unchoreographed but perfectly synchronized dance.

"Hey!"

Their performance ended when David pulled her close to him, then closer. Their lips were scant inches apart. A dance floor was too public for the heedless desire she felt, and yet she would not have wished to be anywhere else. The moment was perfect, in harmony with the universal dance of love. He kissed her emphatically, and they returned to their table amid wild, appreciative applause from the crowd.

"Hey! Hey! Hey!"

He glanced at his watch. "I hate to do this, Jennifer, but I need to make a phone call to Los Angeles."

"Oh, no, David. Please don't, not now."

"I have to." He rose. "This is the only time I can be sure of catching this guy. I'll be back in a minute."

As she watched him slip through the crowd toward the telephones, her vision blurred. Tears? Why? She blinked and focused on the dance floor where three men had linked arms to form a chain. How could David do this to her? She felt as if she'd been raised to the brink of ecstasy, then dropped flat.

"Hey!"

The dancing ended.

Their waiter served dinner and complimented Jennifer on her potential as a belly dancer. And still David had not returned.

She picked the pieces of black olive from her souvlaki and tore off a piece of pita bread. Be patient, she told herself. It wasn't going to be this way forever.

Besides, she wanted a man who was responsible, and she understood that David needed to be totally committed to his work if he intended to be successful. She remembered the twenty-four-hour-a-day effort when she was opening Watt's Up. His dedication was perfectly reasonable, even admirable.

She sighed. But why couldn't life be the way it was in old movies? Why couldn't real-life heroes be competent and romantic, too?

Half an hour passed. Jennifer had turned down advances from two men who'd offered to accompany her while she ate, and had tried to discourage the amorous bouzouki player, who insisted on serenading her.

*This is enough*, she thought as she rose and meandered through the crowded tables. There was a limit to what could be expected, and David had just passed it. Steeling herself, she walked swiftly past the telephones, where David was still rapt in conversation.

"Hey!" he called to her.

"Hey, yourself. I'm going home."

# 7

JENNIFER'S DREAMS that night were in violent Technicolor. Angry reds clashed with an intense blue, and the dream shapes wore ferocious voodoo masks.

Gradually the colors faded to a sunset—a bold slash of scarlet against a pink and yellow sky. The dream ocean was midnight blue. Across frothy waves sailed a fully rigged clipper ship of the eighteen-hundreds. Its sails were striped with gold.

Jennifer flew above the sea, looking down, then falling, floating gently through whispery, silver air. Her purple parachute turned into a feather and whisked away when she landed on the deck of the dream ship. A pirate ship?

Her floor-length dress was dove gray, decorated with cream-colored satin, embroidery and pearls. The scooped neckline dipped dramatically low.

As she strode across the deck, the swarthy pirate brigands stepped aside. Some of them bowed.

The mists parted and she saw David. He posed dramatically at the bow of the ship—king of the roguish pirates, more swashbuckling than Errol Flynn. The salty wind brushed through his hair and rippled the full white sleeves of his pirate shirt. He wore a leather tunic, tight black pants and high leather boots.

There was a sound track in Jennifer's dream—a full orchestra playing "Victory at Sea" in Dolby stereo.

Pirate David leaped from the bow to the deck. With a dashing swagger and a flashing smile he swept her into his arms. "Our love," he said in Clayton Forbes's voice, "is beyond the boundary of time. Timeless."

"How can you say that?" Jennifer responded in her dream voice. She raised her hand. In slow motion she slapped him.

He yanked her to him. Their faces were in a dreamy close-up as he said, "What would you have me do, princess?"

"You must never abandon me again."

"Done!" He found a beautifully engraved, gold pocket watch in the folds of his tunic. With a devil-may-care laugh he flung it overboard. His motley crew cheered. He tilted her back—way back, almost touching the deck—for a kiss. One of his great kisses. Was this a dream?

When she stood upright again, the ship was being attacked by Greek pirates. One of them carried a bouzouki. Their captain was Aziza the belly dancer.

Harriet Kelton perched in the old crow's nest, shouting through a megaphone, "Cut, cut. You are proceeding incorrectly. Trust me. I have years of experience."

Swinging on a mast rope came Philo with his video camera running. Charlie Peyton swung in the opposite direction, aiming his Polaroid.

"Look out," Jennifer shouted.

But they crashed, anyway. And it didn't matter because up, up in the sky Wasp Man soared on silver wing.

"Beware his sting," shouted a pirate with an eye patch.

Jennifer heard a ticking sound, and she looked out to sea. The gold pocket watch was rising from the waters. It had grown larger than the sun. Tick, tick. It was coming closer.

She rose from the depths of unconsciousness and sat upright on her bed. The first words out of her mouth made even less sense than her dream: "You're being too hard on David. Give him another chance."

Then she heard a tick. The killer pocket watch? Then another. Listening carefully, she heard faraway music, something classical.

The sounds seemed to be coming from outside her bedroom window. Tick. There it was again. She climbed out of bed to investigate. It had to be David, she thought. In her groggy state she wondered if he would be wearing a pirate costume.

Tick. She snapped up the shade. Still in his Brooks Brothers suit, David pitched pebbles against the glass. Though her bedroom was on the first floor, her window was seven feet off the ground, and he had placed a small portable radio on the sill. Jennifer laughed. The radio was playing "Victory at Sea."

When he realized that she was watching him, he reacted with a huge, full-force smile. "Jennifer-Juliet, let down your hair."

"That's supposed to be Rapunzel," she murmured.

"Arise, fair Jennifer."

She yanked open the window. "It's after midnight, David."

"Let me in. We have to talk."

"It's one heckuva time to decide that."

"Come on, Jen. Give me another chance."

She eyed him suspiciously. Had he discovered some method of tapping into her dreams? "All right, David. Come around to the front."

By the time she'd slipped a flannel robe over her clinging, silky gown and walked to the front door, he was waiting. She opened the door for him and was greeted by a swirl of bubbles. He dipped a wand into a bubbly bottle and waved another stream of bubbles. Before she could comment, he held a leaded glass kaleidoscope up to her eye.

"David! What are you doing?"

"Special effects."

He was reaching for something else when she grabbed his hand and yanked him inside. "Who do you think you are? George Lucas?"

She closed the door, and silence enveloped them.

"I'm sorry, Jennifer."

"You're pretty sure of yourself, aren't you?" She shuffled into the front room and plopped down on the sofa. Her head felt woolly, and she wished for a cup of coffee. "What if I'd refused to open the door?"

He darted back onto the porch and returned carrying a white paper bag. He dangled it before him like a bribe. "Cappuccino?"

She took the Styrofoam cup, popped off the lid and sipped.

David sat on the opposite end of the sofa and watched her. Her assessment had been dead wrong. He wasn't feeling sure of himself. Not at all. Extravagant gestures weren't part of his usual repertoire, but he knew he couldn't simply apologize. His negligence had been too great.

After he'd paid the tab and left Alexander the Greek's, he'd walked. He *had* to walk; she'd taken the van. First, he was annoyed. Why couldn't she be more understanding? Hadn't he asked her to be patient?

Then heavy-duty guilt set in. How patient did he expect her to be? Sure, his phone call was vital to his business, but their time together was important, too. What if he'd lost her forever?

He'd been afraid to telephone, sure that she'd hang up.

"I had the craziest dream," she said.

He inched nearer to her on the sofa and murmured, "Don't worry, Dorothy. You're back in Kansas now."

"What?"

"*The Wizard of Oz*. There's no place like home."

"This was more of an Errol Flynn epic. Pirate ships and swashbuckling. David, am I being too hard on you? Making too many demands?"

"No," he quickly replied, taking the opportunity to scoot closer to her on the sofa. "When a guy takes you out to dinner, it's not unreasonable to expect him to stay for the meal."

"Good. I always thought my mother was too demanding with my father. If he wasn't fixing up the house, she had him running to a picnic or potluck or church social. The poor man never had a life of his own. Of course, she didn't, either."

"Didn't what?"

"Have an identity beyond wife and mother. When I think about it, nobody in my family was expected to have their own life. We were cogs in the family machine, a preparation for becoming good little cogs in society."

She stretched and yawned. "Please disregard the previous statement. You know I don't make any sense until I've been awake for a while."

"Made sense to me." He moved a little closer on the sofa. "Tell me more. You don't often talk about your family."

"There isn't much to say. We were average. Middle America. Small town. Average."

"How did you get into art?" He was right beside her. "That's not usually a small-town profession."

"Weren't you sitting way over there?" she asked. "How did you get way over here?"

"I crept."

"Well, you can creep your way right back. We've got to settle this scheduling problem we seem to have, and I can't when you're breathing down my neck."

"Like this?" He rested his hand on her opposite shoulder, turning her toward him, and breathed soft kisses along the slender column of her throat.

A tiny thrill slipped through her before she firmly pushed him away. "Don't try to get out of this."

"I'm not trying to get out of anything," he said. "I'm trying to get into—"

"David, I'm serious. We have to set priorities."

"You bet." He unfastened the sash on her robe and slid his hand inside. He cupped her breast. "This is number one."

"For pity's sake, stop it." Drawing upon every ounce of her willpower, she pushed his hand away.

"I meant it, Jennifer. You are number one. You're my life. Making a documentary is my livelihood."

"I don't know. It just seems there are a lot of times when Wasp Man comes first."

"Not in my heart." He sat up straight on the sofa. His attitude was direct and sincere as he clasped both her hands in his. "There might also be times when your business comes first. Like the art fair that kept you from coming to Malibu Beach with me when I first left."

"That's true." She gazed into his gentle gray eyes. "What are we going to do about it?"

"Falling in love doesn't mean we have to stop living. We'll have to deal with each situation as it comes up. I was wrong tonight. My behavior was unforgivable, but I'm asking you to forgive me."

If she stared any longer into his eyes, Jennifer was in danger of hypnotizing herself, losing herself in the reflected depths of his gray irises. "I was so angry," she said. "And so hurt. I feel like you're taking me for granted, and we don't even have a committed relationship."

"We don't?"

"We've never spoken about it."

"Right now it's impossible to make definite plans. It's too early."

## Seems Like Old Times 117

"Or too late. Or too long. Or too short." She broke eye contact with him. "When is the right time, David?"

"What difference does it make? Someday and somewhere. Do we have to have a specific time and place?"

"I need something definite. I mean, what are we? Betrothed lovers? Going steady? Friends? A casual affair?"

"Does it matter? You know that I love you."

She was stunned. She tried to recall if he'd ever told her before, and she drew a blank. Either her brain had ceased functioning, or this was a very important moment. She hadn't been waiting to hear those three little words. But now that they had been spoken, hearing them made all the difference in the world. "You love me?"

He nodded. "I love you. And for the life of me, I cannot define that feeling for you. I only know that it exists."

"I think I know what you mean," she said, suddenly shy. "Because I love you, too."

These mutual declarations seemed sweet and innocent to Jennifer. Like an old-fashioned courtship or the tender stirrings of first love.

"My dream told me to give you another chance," she said.

He leaned closer to her and whispered, "Let's hear it for the dream."

His kiss was exploratory, gentle. He loved her. His tongue slipped through her lips, adoring the soft, warm flesh inside her mouth. He breathed in the sleepy scent of her. Lovely. His hands followed the smooth contours of her torso. Lovable.

Instinctual need swept through him, and he could no longer restrain his passion. Fiercely he kissed her, needing to be close to her, so close that they shared the same breath, the same heartbeat.

His powerful desire met and communed with a spark that flickered within her. She knew that before the night was through, that flame would become an all-consuming conflagration, but she wanted to prolong the pleasure.

"David, I dreamed you were a pirate."

He pulled away from her, looking surprised. "What?"

"You know, a pirate king." She reclined against the arm of the sofa, her arms draped gracefully above her head, and challenged him. "Ravish me."

His closed-mouth smile did not show his perfect teeth, but his dimples deepened. "I think I'm going to like this dream."

"Take off your jacket," she said. "And unfasten the buttons on your shirt."

His white shirt was not cut in the flowing fullness she'd seen in her dream, but he made a dashing figure with his shirt unbuttoned in a deep V. The warm flesh of his chest and the wide swath of curling black hair contrasted with the crisp white cotton.

"Avast," he said as he hoisted her off the sofa and carried her to the bedroom, piratically nuzzling the softness of her unbound breasts. He swaggered the last few steps and dropped her on the bed in a sitting posture. "And now, me fine lady, the true ravishment may begin."

With teasingly rough gestures he whipped off her flannel robe and reached for the neck of her gown. She grabbed his hands before he could rip the delicate material. "Watch it, Long John Silver. This is an expensive gown."

"Well, yo-ho-ho, and a bottle of Perrier." He loomed above her, fists on his hips. "You want me to be some sissy kind of pirate?"

"Maybe it would be safer to go with the special effects," she mused aloud, tweaking a curl of hair on his chest. "Do you still have your soap bubbles?"

"No way, me fine lady." He wiggled his eyebrows and leered. "I'm the captain of this fantasy."

## Seems Like Old Times

From his expression she imagined David, the pirate king, swinging from the chandeliers, brandishing his rapier more expertly than the fabled Errol Flynn. Jennifer laughed, leaned back on the pillows and held out her arms to him.

He lowered himself on top of her, and the fantasy turned to passionate reality. His mouth covered her laughter, demanding and magically fulfilling her. His tongue licked the soft recesses of pink flesh within her mouth.

When he drew away, her breath came in heavy gasps. Her eyes glazed, out of focus, as she stared up at him. He was so handsome, she thought, so magnificently male.

His lips blazed a path down her throat, and Jennifer slipped her hands beneath his shirt, caressing his warmth. Likewise, he sought her nakedness, sliding aside the silky material of her gown to fondle her breasts, bringing the sensitive nipples to unbearable tautness. Under his expert touch she felt herself melting and expanding simultaneously.

His fingers climbed the inside of her thigh, tantalizing her to a throbbing state of readiness. "More ravishing?" he gasped.

"No more. I can't take any more."

"That's good." He swallowed hard. "Because this pirate is going to have a limp sword in about two minutes."

While she wriggled out of her gown, he unbuckled his swash and took off his trousers.

The meeting of their naked flesh provoked long, satisfied moans from both of them. Teasing foreplay was all well and good, Jennifer thought, but she wanted more from him. She parted her thighs and guided him within.

They joined in perfect synchronization, arching and thrusting. Like the eternal tides, their rocking motion created ethereal, primitive waves of excitement as he kept a constant rhythm. When he'd brought her nearly to her peak, he shifted slightly, awakening yet another sensitivity deep within her.

And she moved with him, her body responding to the most subtle nuance of his touch. They balanced on their sides, still joined. She rose above him, trembling and fevered from the heat generated by the energy of their joined flesh. Finally, she could love no more.

With a last shuddering moan she collapsed beneath him and sank into her own special quiet, reveling in the radiant sensations he'd awakened within her.

She sighed and smiled at her pirate king.

"I love you," he said.

"Me, too."

This treasured moment was perfect. There was nothing more that could be said. Jennifer nestled comfortably in the crook of his arm and slept.

HER ALARM CLOCK WENT OFF at seven forty-five. She hit the Sleep button with a practiced swat and flopped back on the pillow.

David was already up, dressed and ready to go. He leaned over her, kissing her lightly. "I'll be back in an hour."

"Great," she mumbled. Opening one eye, she said, "Where are you going?"

"Big day, Jennifer. We're going to start filming. You still want to come, don't you?"

"You bet." She yawned. "I'm real excited."

She looked sleepy-eyed, languid and wonderful. He was tempted to stay here and help her awaken, but duty called. He had a mental list a mile long of things that needed to be done before they headed up to Conifer.

He hopped into Jennifer's van, turned the key in the ignition and chugged away from the curb. Not much pickup, David thought as he shifted into second gear. What did he expect from an old Chevy van? He flexed his fingers on the steering wheel, yearning for the speed and fingertip control of his Porsche.

When he moved to Malibu Beach, David had sold his beloved green sports car to Tom, the guy he was staying with. It was small consolation that Tom had agreed to sell it back. David knew he couldn't afford it until he'd made a bankable profit on this documentary—probably sometime in the next millenium.

He'd figured the budget down to the tiniest detail. On paper the project was comfortably financed, but it was always wise to include a cushion and to expect overruns. Especially on a first-time venture.

Frugality was logical, he thought, and intelligent. But it wasn't any comfort. He wanted his Porsche back.

He drove to Tom's, changed into comfortable Levi's and a red sweater, telephoned Harriet to confirm that they would arrive at ten o'clock and checked with Philo to verify that he had the right kind of lights for indoor photography.

"I have a question," Philo drawled. "Who's the director on this epic?"

"Right now?" David asked.

"No, a week from next Thursday. Of course, right now."

"I am."

An eloquent pause transmitted through the telephone wires before Philo said, "Do you have any experience?"

"No, I don't."

David didn't intend to defend himself. He wasn't sure if the decision to act as his own director was wise, but he figured this documentary wasn't like a feature film where actors needed to be rehearsed and scenes blocked out. The real complexity would come when they were editing the pieces into a whole, and David's budget provided for an excellent technician to handle that process. At this point he'd decided to save by being his own director.

"If it's necessary," he reassured Philo, "I'll hire a director. Actually, I was counting on your skill as a cameraman and Beth's excellent script to carry us through."

"Nice philosophy, Dave. We'll see if it works."

David snarled as he hung up the telephone. Philo and his constant cynicism. The man was a pain in the rear. Still, David had assessed his clips and reviewed his portfolio. Obnoxious or not, Philo was a competent, even excellent, craftsman. And David didn't want to waste time looking for anyone else.

He hurried out the door to the van. Likewise, there wasn't time to worry about Philo's attitude. Was he going to cause trouble? Or not? Jennifer would know, he thought with a grin. She was good at reading people.

And that wasn't all she was good at doing.

By the time he'd pulled into her driveway, David had mentally savored the multitude of Jennifer's attributes. He raced up to her front door, rang the bell and waited. He rang the bell again.

Wearing her flannel robe, she pushed open the door and waved him inside with her free hand. The other hand clutched a coffee mug. Unfortunately, he thought, punctuality was not among her finer qualities.

"I know what you're thinking. I've already showered, and it's only going to take me two minutes to dress."

"Fine." He held up his wristwatch. "Can I start timing you now?"

"Don't be a jerk, David."

"You promised you'd be ready."

"Did I? I can't remember. Surely you can't hold me to a promise I can't even remember."

"One minute and fifty seconds."

"Oh, all right."

She set down her coffee mug and dashed into the bedroom. He heard drawers being opened and closed. There was a crash and a muffled curse as she apparently stumbled over something. Nonetheless, in precisely two minutes she reappeared dressed in an oversized white shirt splotched with bright blue, yellow and red and a pair of jeans. She wore rubber-soled Loafers without socks.

"You look very artsy," he said.

"And prompt," she reminded him. "Answer me a question."

"Shoot."

"How did this lodge happen to end up in Colorado? Why not California?"

"As a former banker, I would remind you that the property costs here are considerably lower than on the coast."

"That makes sense. Is that the reason?"

"As somebody who knows something about cinema history, I would inform you that Denver was the first Hollywood. In the early nineteen-hundreds one of the studios—I think it was Vitagraph—and Mack Sennett made a bunch of those fifteen-minute silent Westerns and comedies here."

"Really?"

"Why not? Back then they did a lot of outdoor shooting, and we have terrific sunshine in Colorado."

"Why didn't they stay?"

He glanced at her and grinned. "It snowed."

"So that's why the industry moved to Hollywood, but it doesn't really explain why The Lodge is here."

"It does in a roundabout way. Mack Sennett took a few star-struck youngsters to Hollywood with him. Among them were Harriet Kelton's parents. Years later, after their darling daughter established herself in film, her parents moved back here and opened The Lodge on their own property."

"The Lodge belongs to Harriet?"

He nodded. "The Lodge and about fifty acres more."

"Well, then," Jennifer said. "She is one of a rarefied breed—a Colorado native in her seventies."

The rest of the drive continued to be easygoing and pleasurable. The mountain scenery on this spectacular, sunny September morn was beautiful. Their conversation was lighthearted and relaxed. But it was more than that. The night before they had finally taken the opportunity to talk. Both Jennifer and David felt more secure in their relationship. Being in love was comfortable and special.

# 8

AS THE VAN BOUNCED along the graded gravel road leading to The Lodge, Jennifer yawned and gazed contentedly at the forested land on the north side of the road. Though it was early September, some of the aspen leaves were already turning gold. On the opposite side of the road a maize-tinted meadow of dry grass stretched toward jumbled formations of adobe-colored rock and boulders.

The variant textures of weed, pine bough and stone appealed to Jennifer. "I wish I'd brought my sketchbook," she said. "Then I could drift off quietly into the woods while you and Philo do the filming."

"I've been meaning to talk to you about your old pal Philo. Is it just me, or does he hate the entire human race?"

"They key to understanding Philo," she explained, "is to remember that he's married to Beth."

David gave her a questioning one-eyebrow-raised glance. "Come again?"

"You see, Beth is sweet and sensitive and thoughtful."

"And Philo is the opposite." He nodded.

"Left to himself, Philo would probably be an average guy, but since he's around Beth all the time, he has to compensate. It's like his caustic attitude equalizes her lovability."

"What if it's the other way around?" David asked. "What if Philo's pessimism is real and Beth's sweetness is a balance?"

"I don't think so," she said. "There have been too many times when Philo's secret pleasantness sneaks out."

She recalled a birthday present from Philo—a beautiful framed photograph of the detailed woodworking on her front porch. The present hadn't come gift wrapped. In fact, she wouldn't have known it was from Philo except for his tiny signature in the corner. "He reminds me of Grumpy in *Snow White and the Seven Dwarfs*—all bluster but kind underneath."

"I hope so," David said. "Otherwise, this filming is going to be miserable."

"Besides, if he were really obnoxious, Beth would dump him."

"Sweet Beth?" David chuckled. "I can't imagine that."

"For your information, laughing boy, sweet is not synonymous with stupid."

"I love the way you explain things. There's no logic, but somehow it sounds right."

As he parked the van and came around to her side to open her door, Jennifer made a quick study of the light and shadow on The Lodge. Standing tall and pale amid its forest sentinels of pine and spruce, the wood frame building exuded an aura of picturesque serenity. Again she wished that she'd remembered her sketchbook.

"Philo's here already," David observed, pointing out the beat-up Volvo station wagon. "Let's hustle."

"You go ahead." Climbing out of the van, she stretched in the sunlight. "I think I'll take a little stroll."

"That sounds suspiciously like exercise."

"Egad! It does. But this way I don't have to help you unload the lights." She went up on tiptoe to give him a little peck on the cheek. "Go on, David. I'll catch you and despicable Philo later."

Feeling as if the day were a lovely unscheduled holiday, she struck off along the well-trodden path leading into the forest. She meandered past several small white cabins—minia ure replicas of The Lodge—and went farther where the path narrowed through the blanket of pine needles and the drying leaves of autumn.

It was a glorious morning, she thought, with blue sky above and sunlight so bright its rays seemed like a palpable force embracing the heavy conifer boughs. Jennifer couldn't think of a time when she'd felt so carefree.

She followed the path to a clear, rippling stream and hunkered down beside it, watching the diamond sheen reflecting off the swift-moving water. The rushing sound permeated her, making her feel clean and fresh and new.

She heard a rustling sound behind her and stood, confronting a gray-haired woman dressed in jeans and a flannel shirt. "Good morning," Jennifer said. "Are you from The Lodge?"

"I am now," the woman said. "But I used to be from Ohio."

"Me, too." Jennifer's response was friendly, but the woman remained taciturn. "The forests there are very different, aren't they?"

"Are you with those documentary people?"

"Kind of."

"I can tell you're an Ohio gal. Being out here in the forest instead of in The Lodge shows that you've got some common sense."

The woman gave a cryptic smile, turned and retreated down the path. Her posture was very erect, and she walked with an arm-swinging, vigorous step.

"Nice meeting you," Jennifer mumbled to herself.

The silhouette of the tall woman striding resolutely through the forest formed a clear, strong image in Jennifer's mind. It reminded her of her mother, marching unstoppably through life. Her mother had also been tall, a real authority figure, capable of stepping over or smashing through any obstacle.

Jennifer found a comfortable rock by the stream and sat watching the shimmering waters. The incongruity of her proper, always correct mother being like anyone from The Lodge amused her. Her mother never had any use for actors or artistic frivolity. Jennifer could almost hear her mother's flat accent in the rushing of springwater over stone.

"Nothing wrong with being artistic," her mother had told her. "But you need to make a living, as well, find a steady career."

Jennifer picked up a pebble and tossed it into the stream. It disappeared without a ripple.

Her father's voice rose from the stream's current to harmonize with her mother's. "Grow up, Jennifer. Learn to take care of yourself."

Jennifer mouthed the remembered woe of both parents. "What will Jennifer do when she's sixty-five? We won't be here forever to take care of her."

They were gone.

Her memories went silent.

If only her parents were still alive, they could have seen that she'd turned out all right. Now when it was too late, Jennifer had become the sort of responsible citizen that they had wanted her to be. It made her sad to realize that she'd never made her peace with them. They had died believing she was an irresponsible child who would probably come to a bad end.

"Time to go back," she said aloud.

Her memories shadowed her enjoyment of the morning. She rose and shivered. Perhaps it was just as well that she'd left her sketchbook at home.

On her way back she passed several other people. They were all polite, pleasant and peaceful. Maybe, Jennifer thought wistfully, her parents would have turned out like them. But it was doubtful. This was a retirement village of former actors—artistic, creative creatures. Her mother and father would have felt more at home in a settlement of Martians.

*Martians,* she thought as she approached The Lodge. *They've landed.* Standing on the front lawn were three figures—a handsome, silver-haired gentleman dressed as Superman and two bizarre, scaly creatures with webbed feet and reptilian heads.

"Good morning," Jennifer said, congratulating herself on not bursting into laughter. "Are they filming inside?"

"Are you with them?" Superman asked.

She nodded, and one of the reptiles took off his head. "I'm getting out of this damn uniform," he said. "This was all Charlie Peyton's idea."

"Wait a minute," Superman said. He held up the Polaroid photo that Charlie had snapped the first time he saw Jennifer. "You're the lady we were supposed to meet. It's Jennifer Watt, isn't it?"

"Yes, it is. I am." She shook hands with Superman and slapped flippers with the other two. "Is this about movie memorabilia for my store?" she guessed. "Charlie Peyton's idea?"

"It is," said Superman. "Charlie told us that you might be interested in purchasing some of these old costumes."

"Hope you decide quick," said the headless reptile. "Because I feel like a damn fool."

"Me, too" came a muffled voice from beneath the other's head.

"Well, take your head off," Superman said. "It is pretty silly-looking. We never get this stuff out excepting for Halloween."

"Halloween," Jennifer said thoughtfully. Why hadn't Charlie Peyton come up with that idea? She studied the costumes. Not only were they original, but also they had an aura of authenticity. "Would you gentlemen be willing to rent these outfits? For Halloween costumes?"

"You bet," Superman said. "This junk isn't doing us any good packed away in trunks. This Superman costume is the newest—belonged to my son, the stuntman, who worked on the movie. And it still stinks of mothballs."

The fully dressed reptile said something that sounded like, "We could all use the extra bucks."

Jennifer's mind was racing. Halloween costumes. But, she reminded herself, everybody—from drugstores to professional theater companies—offered Halloween costumes. "We need an advertising gimmick."

"Maybe something to do with movie memorabilia," Superman said. "Costumes of the stars."

"Not bad," she said appraisingly.

Unfortunately, Jennifer's shop couldn't support an expensive advertising campaign. Maybe one or two newspaper ads. And flyers. She studied the threesome. If they went around in costume to pass out flyers, she could certainly garner some good, positive publicity. "Is there any chance," she asked, "that you three could make personal appearances for a limited promotion? Maybe visit a couple of day-care centers? Or a hospital?"

The headless reptile grinned widely. "In spite of what we're wearing, you are looking at three hams."

"Personal appearances?" Superman preened, gently touching his wavy silver hair. "No problem."

The other reptile bobbed his head.

The door to The Lodge swung open, and David stepped out onto the porch. He looked around with a harassed, glassy-eyed gaze. "We're ready for the swamp monsters," he announced.

As the swamp monsters filed past him, foot flippers slapping the floor, David noticed Jennifer. He came quickly down the stairs from the porch.

"Is something the matter?" she asked.

"Everything is the matter."

Superman swirled his cape for an exit. "Welcome to show biz, kids." He tossed a parting comment over his shoulder. "Don't worry. It'll only get worse."

"Thanks," David growled sarcastically. "I needed that."

Jennifer studied David's expression. His eyebrows were drawn down, his jaw was tense and the lobes of his ears were bright pink. If she were writing his emotional state as a recipe, it would include anger, confusion, hysteria, concern and a pinch of excitement.

"I hate this kind of disorganization. Nobody is paying attention. Drives me crazy." His fists were clenched. "Jennifer, you've got to help me."

"Love to. Could you be a tiny bit more specific? What's the problem?"

"Them." He pointed toward The Lodge. "All of them. We're supposed to shoot a couple of simple interviews with people who knew Uncle Clayton. Reminiscences. Harriet is the interviewer, and it's supposed to be casual and off-the-cuff."

"I take it that's not what is happening."

"Hah!" David paced away from her and charged back, listing his frustrations on his fingers. "Your friend Philo has done nothing but gripe and pick nits from his beard. Gloria, the plump lady from the kitchen, is feeding everybody. Harriet won't talk about any movies but her own. And, for some unknown reason, they're all wearing costumes."

"Ouch. I think the costumes might be my fault. You see, Charlie Peyton had suggested—"

"Don't mention that name to me. He's wearing the Wasp Man outfit, and he keeps darting around stinging everybody."

Jennifer bit the inside of her cheeks to keep from giggling. "Is that all?"

He grabbed Jennifer's hand and dragged her toward The Lodge. "You're good with people. You talk some sense into them."

The nearer they got to the scene David had described, the louder the babble of voices and laughter grew. "Do you hear them?" David asked.

"They sound cheerful."

"Why shouldn't they be?" he groused. His earlobes were now flaming crimson. "I'm the one renting the equipment. I'm the one financing this party."

He flung open the door and marched her inside.

The formerly charming parlor was in chaos. In addition to the swamp monsters there were three Southern belles in hoop skirts, Lionel as a gaunt Sherlock Holmes, an octogenarian tap-dancing duo and assorted others in street clothes. The photographer's lights were focused on the Victorian-style sofa where Harriet sat primly, studying Beth's script.

Philo was sprawled in one of the director's chairs. He glanced up as they entered. "Hey, Mr. Producer, the swamp monsters want to know if they should take off their heads."

"I'll tell them what they can do with their heads," David muttered.

Charlie Peyton came buzzing through the room, spied Jennifer and waved. "Hey, Jennifer, did you talk to Superman?"

Jennifer shushed him. "Not now, Charlie."

"What?" He buzzed up to her. "What?"

In a loud tone Jennifer never expected dwelt within David Constable, he bellowed, "Quiet. Everybody settle down."

## Seems Like Old Times      133

There was a lull, and the crowd turned toward him. Charlie Peyton prudently exited.

"Tell them to clear this room," Jennifer prompted.

"Get out!" he yelled. "All of you except Harriet. Get out."

Jennifer stepped forward. "As you all know, we need quiet while we're doing these interviews. It would be greatly appreciated if you waited for your call outside."

"Not on the porch!" David roared.

"Since we can still pick up the sound from the porch," Jennifer translated, "please move farther out, onto the lawn."

"Now!" He made frantic, shooing motions. "Let's move it."

The assembled group stood before him like a tableau. Jennifer looked toward Lionel, who was pointedly ignoring David and lighting his pipe. She made a guess at the problem. "Did you all know that David is the director?"

"Oh, no, dear girl," Lionel corrected in his best Sherlockian tones. "David is the producer."

"*And* the director."

There was a general murmuring as they digested this bit of information. Jennifer glanced over at David, who was practically frothing at the mouth. "You'll all understand. He's a bit temperamental."

"Honey, you don't have to tell us," drawled one of the Southern belles. "We've worked with Hitchcock and Howard Hawks and Erich Von Stroheim."

Before they had a chance to launch their complaints, Jennifer intervened. "You've all worked with his explosive type of director," she cajoled. "If you'll all step outside, we'll discuss our format for the interviews."

Appeased, they trailed after Jennifer like the rats of Hamelin following the Pied Piper. She propelled them a good distance from The Lodge to a picnic table beneath a majestic spruce. Lionel took a position by her side. "Very nicely done," he complimented.

"Thank you, I'm used to working with artistic people." She looked around at the assembled group. "Lionel, could you get their attention?"

He shouted for quiet, and Jennifer hopped up on the picnic table to address them. "I would like to make a proposition to each of you. This has nothing to do with the documentary filming."

She explained about renting Halloween costumes and the possibility of selling movie memorabilia in her store. "If I open a movie memories section, I want it to be different. Not just posters, but personal souvenirs."

"A lacy fan from *Gone With the Wind*?" asked a belle.

"Exactly," Jennifer confirmed.

"Maybe a half-burned black candle from *Dracula*," suggested Lionel.

"Tap shoes worn in *Kiss Me Kate*," said a tap dancer as she executed a spry shuffle-off-to-Buffalo.

"Wonderful," Jennifer said. "What I need is for each of you to select things you want to sell and determine a price."

"How can we tell what the stuff is worth?" asked a swamp monster.

"I'm not sure," Jennifer answered.

"Well, then?"

A nostalgic warmth welled up inside her. There were so many memories among these people, so many charming memories. "To someone like me," she said, "many of your souvenirs are priceless. You were the people who helped shape my dreams, my fantasies. I've spent so many hours watching you, all of you, and you've enriched my life. You'll have to decide the price."

As she looked at the people surrounding her, she recognized a kinship among them. "I don't think of this as merchandising," she said. "It's a way we can spread and share these dreams."

"But we are going to get paid, aren't we?" the swamp monster demanded.

"We better," agreed a belle. "Ain't no kind of a dream if it don't make money."

"Sometimes," Jennifer mused aloud, "the most precious dreams are free. However, rest assured that I will pay for whatever is sold. On a consignment basis." She hopped down from her makeshift podium. As the assembled group of actors and actresses began discussing possible items that could be offered for sale, Jennifer relaxed in the warm sunshine. Lionel sat beside her at the picnic table. He'd removed his deerstalker hat and his cape, but he still fiddled with his meerschaum pipe.

"Good show," he complimented her again. "You have a flair for public speaking, dear. Ever considered a career in movies?"

"No, I'm an artist."

Jennifer blinked. *I'm an artist?* Was she? She'd spent the better part of two years denying her artistic nature.

"Elementary," Lionel said. "That's why you can communicate with us."

"But I'm also a retailer," she said firmly. She certainly couldn't deny that facet of her identity, especially not when all these other people would soon be depending upon her to merchandise and sell their memorabilia. "Lionel? Could you keep an eye on things out here? I'd like to see how the interviews are going."

"Leave it to me."

She hurried across the lawn and into The Lodge. Harriet was interviewing good old Charlie Peyton. Philo watched through the stationary camera lens. David, who had cooled to merely steaming, slumped in a corner of the room. She beckoned to him, and he followed her into the foyer.

"Thank you," he whispered, taking both her hands in his and raising them to his lips.

"You're welcome," she whispered back. "I know all you big-time movie executives have ulcers, but I didn't think you needed to start on yours the first day."

"Philo was right," David admitted. "I need a director. I thought I could save some money by doing it myself."

"How are the interviews going?"

"All right. Harriet is still pushing her own career, but it can be cut."

"You see," Jennifer said, trying to bolster his ego. "You're not hopeless as a director. You were successful with Harriet."

"Not me. It's Philo. The two of them seem to be operating on the same wavelength. She's even flirting with him."

Jennifer gave him a wink. "She'd better not start on you."

"It wouldn't matter." He surrounded her with his arms. "I'm a sweet, old-fashioned, one-woman kind of guy."

She moistened her lips. "I know."

Before he could execute the awaited kiss, Philo shouted from the other room, "I'm out of film. Do you want more on Charlie?"

"That ought to be enough," David shouted back. He refocused his attention on Jennifer.

"Are you sure?" Philo whined. "I could reload the video camera for another interview. Or we could go outside with the 16 mm."

With a sigh David released her. "Duty calls."

As he returned to the room where Philo was filming, Jennifer had a premonition. If she wanted to spend time with David, it would be necessary to get involved in his documentary.

*The price of loving David,* she thought, *might be very steep in terms of time.*

She glanced around the corner in time to see him, bending to peer through the lens of the stationary video camera. He straightened, stretched and ran his hand through his hair.

Jennifer grinned. He was worth it.

## 9

TWO WEEKS LATER, Jennifer and David stood in the doorway of her shop, applauding as Philo completed an exterior shot of Harriet Kelton being helped from a Rolls-Royce by a liveried chauffeur. For a woman in her seventies, Jennifer thought, Harriet could get away with showing a lot of leg.

"That ought to do it," David said as he collapsed against the doorframe. *"Fini."*

"Pardon me if I don't order Dom Pérignon." Jennifer rested her hand on his shoulder and massaged it. "But I have heard that line somewhere before."

"When?"

"Yesterday, the day before and the day before that."

"It's been hell, hasn't it?"

"Not always. That picnic in the mountains was fun, especially when Philo was trying to get a dramatic shot and fell into the stream."

"With all the rented camera equipment," David groused. "I'm glad we got that straightened out. No more expensive 16 mm film, not even for exteriors. Everything on good old videotape."

"I agree," she said. "I like watching the instant replays on videotape."

"In movies they're called rushes, Jen."

"Rushes, crushes, whatever." She pushed open the door to Watt's Up and went inside, pulling David along with her. "I liked that expensive dinner you threw for the local PBS television people."

"What else?"

"I've really enjoyed being around the people from The Lodge. Lionel and Gloria and Harriet and the swamp monsters, and even Charlie Peyton, King of the Extras."

She glanced toward the back room of her shop. A neon sign—courtesy of Delilah—hung above the door. It said, Movie Memories, Seems Like Old Times. "I miss the extra storage space," she said. "But after Halloween I should be able to do some rearranging."

"Do you know what I miss?" he asked. "We've been together during the last two weeks, but we're never alone."

"Finally." She slipped her arms around his neck and gave him a seductive wink. "I thought you'd never notice."

He rested his hands on her hips. "I've noticed."

She bit her lip to keep from complaining. She knew how hard he had been working. Since he was struggling to stay within his budget, David compensated by working double time. If someone needed to pick up a package at the airport or make a run to the film-processing lab or fetch coffee, David was there. Every night he poured over long rows of figures in the account books, arranged schedules and studied contracts.

She couldn't expect him to handle one more thing. Their romance had to be put on hold until David's schedule slowed to a reasonable pace. The effort needed for their relationship was physically beyond his capabilities. After all, there were only twenty-four hours in a day.

And he did love her, she reminded herself. There would be a future for them. It was a matter of patience.

"Rosebud," he whispered in her ear.

"What?"

"You're supposed to be intrigued. And fascinated about the ending." He imbued his voice with disappointment. "It worked for Orson Welles in *Citizen Kane*."

"Okay, Orson. Is it going to be a happy ending?"

"That depends," he said. "Is there a full moon tonight?"

"Are you planning to turn into a werewolf?"

"If there's a full moon, Philo wanted to shoot a bit of night footage with Harriet materializing from the darkness. You know, like in that movie she did about the blind woman."

Jennifer pulled away from him. *Patience*, she reminded herself. "What happened to *fini*?" She bustled to the counter and began energetically rearranging the clutter that always seemed to gather by the cash register. If she kept her hands busy, she figured that she might be able to keep her mouth shut. "I thought you were finished shooting for today."

"I am finished shooting. In the daylight."

"Fine, David." Despite her vow to be understanding, she couldn't keep the sarcasm out of her voice. "I'll try to arrange our relationship according to the phases of the moon."

A wisp of guilt skittered across her conscience, but she dismissed it. If she didn't tell him how neglected she felt, how would he know?

"You're upset," he said. "I'm sorry."

"I don't want you to apologize. I miss you, David. I want for you to spend some time with me."

"Why don't you say so?"

"I just did."

"Right, you did. And there'll be another full moon next month. Just like reruns. Jennifer, would you like to go out to dinner and a movie?"

"The last place I want to go is out. Especially out to watch a movie. I want to stay in. With the phone unplugged and the doorbell muffled." She paused. The picture that presented itself in her mind was pleasant, very pleasant. "Maybe a bottle of wine," she said wistfully. "If there has to be a movie, make it a classic on the VCR."

"You got it, lady. I'll pick up the movie. Any preference?"

"Surprise me. As long as it doesn't star Harriet Kelton or any superhero who wears tights."

"You got it." He checked his wristwatch. "I'm late. I'll see you tonight."

"No excuses," she called after him.

At the door he pivoted and grinned. "Jennifer? If there is a full moon, do you mind if I turn into a werewolf?"

"I've always preferred vampires," she said. "They don't shed."

As he waved and dashed out the door, the telephone rang. "Watt's Up. May I help you?"

"Please listen to me," the whispery voice pleaded. "We must leave the past. Think of the future."

"Look," Jennifer said shortly. "This is the fourth time you've called, and you're still not making sense. Tell me what you want, or get off the phone."

There was a pause, a click and the dial tone.

"Weirdo." Jennifer glared at the receiver. "If I hadn't paid a thousand dollars for classified telephone advertising, I'd have this number changed."

The remainder of Jennifer's afternoon was hectic. Lionel and two others from The Lodge came in with more memorabilia items to be priced and displayed. Four potential part-time employees had to be interviewed. There were stacks of filing, tax forms, advertising, and of course, customers.

Jennifer had barely time to rush home, kick off her shoes and sink onto the sofa before the doorbell signaled David's arrival. "It's open," she called out.

Though she knew his day had been equally busy, David sounded fresh and cheerful as he flung open the door and shouted in an absolutely dreadful Cuban accent, "Lucy, I'm home."

"In here, Ricky."

He carried four sacks. While she sprawled, unmoving, he unloaded his treasures. "We have not one, but two, bottles of vino. A Cary Grant movie. An extra large bag of popcorn. And Chinese food."

"Cary Grant?"

"Not too subtle on my part. But I know how to put you in the mood for love."

"Actually—" she dragged herself to a sitting position "—the Chinese food is more stimulating right at the moment."

"You're tired," he deduced as he plopped down next to her. In an instant his teasing became serious. "Have I told you, lately, how terrific you are?"

"Not lately. It's hard to tell me anything when you have a telephone glued to your ear and an airline ticket in your pocket."

"You cut me to the quick, Wasp Woman." He clutched his hands over his heart. "Even workaholics have feelings."

"Is that what you are, David? A workaholic?"

"Sometimes." He slipped an arm around her and gently pulled her toward him. "Whatever I do, I like to do well."

It wasn't until their lips met that Jennifer realized how much she'd missed their lovemaking. His tongue parted her lips and penetrated her mouth, readily awakening her dormant passions. "David," she breathed, "don't ever make me wait again."

"You got that promise, lady." His voice was already husky, thick with emotion. "I'll sign a contract in blood if necessary."

"Don't be gross, just kiss me."

Eyes closed, she surrendered her body to the flood of desire that churned through her. So swiftly, so thoroughly. The caress of his fingertip on her breast brought back the sensual excitement she hadn't thought about—hadn't allowed her-elf to think about—while he was busy with other things. She hadn't expected to be instantaneously aroused. That sort of hormonal rush was reserved for the young, wasn't it?

Apparently not, Jennifer thought, because she found herself reclining on the sofa, dragging him on top of her. Her need for him was desperate. She couldn't imagine being glib or coy. She wanted him. "Now, David," she gasped.

Her fingers fumbled with his belt, and David wordlessly assisted her. Their mutual need was too tremendous for finesse, and they tore away at their buttons, belts, zippers, panty hose, blouse. Damn, there was so much clothing in the way, and her hands felt so clumsy. Finally, they were undressed.

He arranged her on the sofa pillows and straddled her body with his muscular thighs. His nakedness was magnificent. He'd lost weight, she noticed. The muscle was closer to the bone, more finely honed, and his body seemed beautifully primitive, uncivilized.

He entered her, swiftly, fiercely, surmounting the unstoppable passion that roared through them like an avalanche. Only warm. Hot. The friction of his flesh against hers was unbearably hot, and Jennifer gave herself completely to the tumult. Her breath came in ragged gasps.

They rose together, clinging and demanding until neither could withstand another instant's wait. Falling together in a spiral, they were sated.

Such lovemaking, such a burst of impulsive desire, deserved an equally unexpected denouement, and David inadvertently provided the final stroke. He sank beside her on the sofa, struggling to maneuver himself around Jennifer and all the embroidered sofa pillows. His skillful lovemaking had depleted his natural grace, and his movements were heavy, nearly unconscious. Without much ado he maneuvered himself right onto the floor.

"Smooth move," he muttered, massaging that portion of his anatomy that had made hard contact with the naked hardwood floor.

"Cute," she assured him dreamily. "Some people smoke after sex. You fall out of bed."

"In the first place, this isn't a bed. Second, knock it off. The male ego does not leave much room for pratfalls."

"I don't care if you want to play Harpo Marx, beep a car horn and wiggle your eyebrows," she murmured, rolling over to her stomach on the sofa. "You, David Constable, are the most male male I have ever encountered."

He kissed her and looked quizzically into her eyes. "Still hungry?"

She nodded. "Did you bring chopsticks?"

"Ah-so, Missy Jennifer want chop-chop." He tried a Charlie Chan voice as he unloaded the white cartons from the sacks and arrayed them on the coffee table. "Number one chum, he got it all—the flied lice, the velly hot mustard, the sweet-and-sour pork, egg loll, many, many egg loll."

Jennifer stabbed an egg roll with her chopstick and took a huge bite from the end. "Don't get the wrong idea," she said. "I'm not the sort of person who eats off the coffee table, bare naked and dropping crumbs on the sofa."

"You should be ashamed," he cheerfully agreed.

"I'm civilized." She dipped into the container for a chopstickful of sweet-and-sour pork. "I've learned to control my appetites."

"I can tell."

Though the impetuous side of her personality was delighted with this crazy spontaneity, another side was truly appalled. She imagined a tiny version of herself, all dressed in white as it sat on her shoulder and made tsk-tsk noises in her ear. "Honestly," that tidy little self would say, "get dressed, Jennifer. And put the food on plates. We weren't brought up in a barn, were we?"

She dropped a huge dollop of fried rice on the floor and stared at it. Retribution? The problem with spontaneity was that somebody had to sweep up afterward. She rose to her feet. "Time to clean up our act," she said.

"Wait!" He was standing beside her with a fortune cookie in his hand. "Open it now. For luck."

She cracked it open, read and laughed. "I must have gotten your fortune, David. This says that I will take a long journey to an exotic land." She popped the cookie into her mouth. "Doesn't get much more exotic than Malibu Beach."

David read his fortune, "Your dreams will be answered one hundredfold."

"Ponder that," she said, heading toward the bedroom, "while I slip into something more...something."

He slipped into his trousers. *His dreams would be answered.* When he was working at the bank, he seldom indulged in any sort of fantasy whatsoever. His banker's life had progressed nicely, and he didn't want for anything. Now there was so much that he wanted.

Now he could see a wide horizon of possibilities, and he wanted it all.

David leaned back on the sofa and closed his eyes. The house in Malibu Beach was part of his perfect dream state—a home near the ocean. And he needed a livelihood that stimulated his imagination. It had to be producing motion pictures. And he wanted his Porsche back. Most of all, he wanted Jennifer to be a permanent part of his reality and of his dreams.

If everything went smoothly on the Wasp Man documentary, he was certain that he'd be producing another such film for Public Broadcasting Service. And after that another.

Though it had seemed incredibly easy, he'd be near success. He could ask her to share his life. He would be able to support her—even though she'd probably want to keep Watt's Up.

He reread his fortune. *His dreams would be answered.*

Jennifer came back into the room, wearing a flowing robe and carrying plates, napkins and two wineglasses on a lacquered tray. David admired her graceful economy of movement as she swept up the spilled rice and arranged the coffee table so that they could eat without being chaotic. Perhaps, he thought, the most important dream had already been answered. She was there with him, and she loved him.

She knelt on the floor beside the table. "And now, Mr. Fu Manchu, we're going to attempt to be civil. Would you pop the cork and pour the wine?"

"Does this mean I have to put on my shirt?"

"Leave it off." She ogled him with comically exaggerated lust. "Give an old lady something to look at."

"You call yourself an old lady after that performance?" He dutifully opened the wine and filled their glasses. "You could give lessons."

"I never fancied myself a teacher. But I suppose you're right. When you're hot, you're hot."

"Want to watch Cary Grant while we eat?"

"Absolutely. Now there was a man who could give lessons."

David loaded the tape in the VCR and arranged the television stand so that they could eat, talk and watch at the same time. He sat beside her on the sofa and flicked the remote to start the movie. The credits rolled, and David reran the tape, studying the names.

"See that," he pointed out. "My uncle knew practically all of the secondary leads, the cinematographer and the best boy."

"What's a best boy?" she murmured through a mouthful of sweet-and-sour pork.

"This film was in the early fifties," he said, ignoring her question. "And I'll bet it didn't cost a fifteenth of what a similar movie would cost today."

"And a key grip?" she asked. "I've always thought that sounded like somebody who locked up after the movie was over."

"The grip is a sort of handyman," he explained. "The gaffer is an electrician. The best boy is a sort of general production person who does a bit of everything, especially for the gaffer."

"Thanks, I'm impressed."

"I might be learning while I go," David said. "But I am learning."

Still munching her way through the multitude of white cartons of Cantonese Chinese food, she focused on the movie. *Charade*. She'd seen it several times before, and it never failed to entertain her. This was vintage Cary Grant—charming, witty and attractive. "Go for it," she urged a reluctant Audrey Hepburn. "Even if you think he murdered your husband."

"Those were the days," David said.

"They were," she agreed. "Everything was beautiful and somehow innocent."

"And inexpensive."

She glared at him. "I don't want to know the actor's salaries, the production costs and the expense of film, David. I want to enjoy the movie."

"Sorry," he said. "It's on my mind."

She tried to ignore his preoccupation with the mundane process that created movie magic. It was much nicer, Jennifer thought, to believe that the scenes were actually occurring while some fortunate cameraman happened to capture the moments. The illusion was damaged when she considered that this was a script and the actors were following a director's scheme.

To be fair, Jennifer realized that when she studied a painting, the structure and brushwork were evident. David was doing what came naturally. That realization jolted her. When had he become so knowledgeable? Certainly he was still in transition, but she could see that he was on course. David was going to be a producer of film.

"I'm proud of you," she said. "I might seem impatient and cranky, but I'm really proud of your progress."

He did one of his eyebrow-raised looks. "To what do I owe this honor?"

"I realized that you're on your way. You're going to do what you said. You, David Constable, are going to be a movie producer."

"Coming from you, that is high praise." He took her hand and kissed her fingertips. "I trust your intuition, Jennifer."

"Tell me. How soon will you be finished? I mean really finished."

"It's within the foreseeable future. We've shot all the interviews. And I've already started the editing. I can't mess around with it much longer, anyway. I've already spent my projected budget."

"What does that mean?" Her interest became concern. "You are going to be able to finish before you run out of cash, aren't you?"

"No problem. All it really means is that despite all the classes I took and my banking background, it's much more complex to budget in real life than on paper."

"No problem?" she repeated skeptically. "No money is no problem?"

"If I need it, I've got a financial source," he said proudly. Perhaps it wasn't as dramatic as slaying a dragon or battling the ravaging horde, but he was very pleased with his conquest. "There are times when being a former banker has its rewards. Remember that sweet old guy at the Brown Palace?"

"Of course I do. It was Mr. Waldheim. And he owns half of the western slope."

He was taken aback. "I never would have expected you to remember Waldheim."

"When money is concerned, I don't often forget," she said with a wink.

"Anyway, Waldheim has offered me a line of credit from his personal venture capital in case I need extra capital in a hurry. And he didn't even require the house in Malibu Beach as security."

"That's fantastic!"

"I can see the light at the end of the tunnel, Jen. And the light is green."

She gave him a happy little hug and returned her attention to the television screen as Cary Grant struggled with one of the bad guys in rugged hand-to-hand combat. Cary won. And his suit wasn't even wrinkled.

It was too bad, she thought, that in real life the bad guys weren't required to wear black hats. "Are you sure you can trust Mr. Waldheim? Are there any other conditions for repayment?"

"They're good conditions," he said. "When *Wasp Man Speaks* is wrapped up, Waldheim asked me to submit proposals for two educational films about his wife's favorite charity, the Denver Symphony."

"Is that good?"

"It's great. An excellent opportunity to gain more experience while beefing up my credits."

"You're almost a production company, aren't you?"

"Almost." He gazed into her eyes. "It won't be long."

It couldn't happen soon enough for him. He needed the success and prosperity before he would ask her to share his life. And he wanted her as a partner.

"When you're a big-shot movie producer," she asked, "are you going to forget all the little people?"

"Meaning?"

"Are you going to be interested in a nobody retailer who owns an arts and crafts shop in Denver?"

"Jennifer, I'm doing this for us. I want to be able to give you anything your heart desires. I want to shower you with pearls, to carry you off for a weekend in Tahiti."

"No, David." Her voice was very low and serious. "You are doing this for yourself. And that is the way it should be. You can't live your life for other people."

Jennifer turned and watched the movie, but her statement resounded. For her. She couldn't live her life for other people. There was a message in that thought, but before she made the connection, the telephone rang. "Damn," she said. "I forgot to unplug the phones."

"I'll get it," he said.

"Oh, no, you won't. I refuse to have you rushing off for some moonlight filming with Harriet dressed as a wraith." She grabbed for the phone. "Hello?"

"It's Philo. Jennifer, is David there?"

She purposely drawled out her response. "Lovely weather we've been having. Did you have a message for David?"

"I don't know what game you're playing, Jennifer, but I need to talk with your buddy."

"He's unable to come to the phone. Tell me."

"Okay." She could almost hear Philo grinding his teeth. "Tell Mr. Producer that he's got one hell of a crisis. There was an accident in the editing room."

Without another word she passed the telephone to David. What if all the film had been destroyed? Could David procure financing to cover reshooting the entire documentary?

She watched him, seeing his body tense as he listened. The light in his eyes was hard and angry.

"An accident?" he repeated.

# 10

IT WASN'T as bad as it sounded. It was worse.

The accident had been a small fire in the basement area at Vids 'R' Us, the sound and video studio where the *Wasp Man Speaks* documentary was being edited. Though the fire had been quickly extinguished by the automatic triggering of the overhead sprinkler system, some of the videotapes had been destroyed.

David shoved past the departing firemen, and Jennifer followed in his wake. They ran to the basement. There was nothing they could do but stand and stare at the soggy, charred videocassettes.

He gripped her hand, and she felt the anger coursing through him. Anger and despair, Jennifer thought as she agonized with him. He had come so close.

Philo whipped through the door into the small basement room. His lips were drawn in a tense line. "Nobody can explain our little accident," he said. "The cop who was here and the firemen said it wasn't big enough to merit an arson investigation."

"What's David supposed to do?" Jennifer demanded.

"File it on insurance."

"But these tapes are irreplaceable," she snapped. "There isn't any explanation? Nothing at all?"

"An accident," Philo said disgustedly. "Or a prank. Maybe cigarettes. A fire in a trash can. Wanda smokes a lot, but she's real careful."

"Wanda?" Jennifer asked.

"The woman helping me with the editing," Philo explained.

"Wanda Cotterel is the technician, the engineer who makes the cuts where we want them," David corrected tersely. "Philo is helping her."

The antipathy that had always existed between the two men had accelerated. Jennifer saw it in their eyes and heard it in their voices.

"What film was in here?" David demanded.

"It's a videotape. And you can see it, can't you?"

"Philo," David thundered. "What did we lose?"

"Not much of the new stuff. We were working on that in the studio upstairs. What we lost were your personal cassettes of *Wasp Man*."

"All right." David let out the breath he was holding. "Is that all?"

"Isn't that enough? Weren't these the only copies?"

"I returned the original kinescopes to the producers," David said. "They've given their blessing to this project, so I'm sure I can get copies from them."

Jennifer let out a cheer and threw her arms around his neck. "You're not wiped out."

"Not completely. But this is going to be an extra expense. We've lost film, and we're going to lose time in figuring out what we've still got and what we need."

"How are you going to decide what you need?" Philo asked peevishly. "You've got to replace all of them."

"I can't afford that. I know all the *Wasp Man* stories from beginning to end. I'll have to work more closely with Wanda in deciding what we need."

"What about Beth's script?"

"We'll have to adjust," David said. Jennifer could hear the suppressed rage in his voice as he continued, "I can't go any higher over budget. I've made agreements, signed contracts and there are certain deadlines which must be met."

"Is that so?"

"It is." His fingers curled into fists, but he kept his tone level. "No matter what we've lost, we can't shoot any more new stuff. None at all."

"Hey, David," Philo sneered. "I'm an artist. If I need to shoot more film, I will."

"Don't push me. Not now."

The two men were squaring off for a fight. Given Philo's attitude, Jennifer was nearly ready to step aside and allow David to wipe the floor with him. Nearly, but not quite.

"Stop it," she snapped. "You're both upset about this, but fighting isn't going to solve anything."

"I'm not upset," Philo said. "As far as I'm concerned, that *Wasp Man* junk is no loss. We didn't need it, anyway."

"A lucky accident?" David growled.

"You might say that."

In two strides David covered the space between them. The difference in their size was never more apparent than when David towered over Philo, physically dominating him. "I'm going to ask this once, Philo. Only once. Did you start this fire?"

"What?"

"You heard me."

"You're full of it, David," he said, not backing down an inch. "I don't work that way."

Jennifer believed him—not because she'd known him for years and his wife was her best friend, but she believed that Philo's artistic egoism would not allow him to destroy anything that might augment his final creation.

David turned to her, and she sensed that he was waiting for her judgment. So many times he'd used her as a sounding board to gauge the emotions behind the actions, but this was the first occasion that she realized the consequences of her perception.

"David," she said, "Philo didn't do it."

"Somebody did." He moved away from Philo. "But I don't understand why. We're not working with classified material here. Why would somebody want to stop a Wasp Man documentary?"

"Maybe they want to stop you," Philo said. "I'm sure you've got enemies, people you turned down for loans."

"Or maybe they're after you, Philo," Jennifer put in.

The cameraman looked genuinely shocked. Then his eyebrows lowered. He seemed to be reviewing an enemy list of his own. "You know, Jennifer, that's possible. I've done some outstanding work on some of the stuff with Harriet. This documentary is going to move me creatively. You think it might be professional jealousy?"

"It's possible. Who knew about your work?"

"Everybody. I've told everybody."

"Then you don't leave me much choice," David said. "You're off this project, Philo."

"You're not going to dump me."

"The hell I'm not. You've been condescending, obnoxious, aggressive and pushy."

Philo looked to Jennifer to talk sense into David, but she could only shrug. "From what I've seen, he's right."

"That's real loyal, Jennifer," Philo snarled. "I warned you from the beginning that this guy was going to hurt you. He's going to mess up your life. But you're on your own now, lady. Don't come crying to me."

Philo pivoted and started toward the door. Then he stopped. Jennifer was glaring at his back, boring holes through him. How dare he presume to protect her? And how could she have been so wrong about Beth's husband? In spite of all Philo's bluster, Jennifer had always thought of him as a sensitive person. As she watched, he seemed to deflate. His thin shoulders slumped. There was something that was keeping him from walking out that door.

Still facing away from them, Philo mumbled, "I'm sorry."

His words reverberated among them for an instant before Philo spun around and said more loudly, "I'm sorry."

"Your apology is accepted," David said.

"Am I back on the project?"

"We've had our differences," David said. "And we'll probably never be friends. But I have to acknowledge your expertise, your talent and your skill. You've taught me a helluva lot."

Jennifer didn't think it was possible, but Philo actually grinned. He crossed to David and held out his hand. "You're not as big an asshole as I thought."

They clasped hands. "Welcome back," David said.

Jennifer's eyes misted over, and she dashed away the moisture before either of the men noticed. Men, she thought. Two minutes ago they were ready to rip each other's throats out; now they were the very picture of friendship. Did all of their relationships have to be tested by fire?

Philo went over to her. He took her hands in his. "I'm sorry, Jennifer."

"You should be." She hugged him. "It's all right."

"Okay," David said, rubbing his hands together. "My guess is that this wasn't an accident. I'll file my insurance claim, but the best revenge is to complete our project on schedule."

"I'll call Wanda," Philo offered. "We can start extra early tomorrow."

"Whoa," David said. "I have to pay Wanda and I can't afford to bring her in here any earlier. In fact, I might have to cut back on her hours."

"Maybe I could help," Jennifer offered.

The two men turned and looked at her. Philo rolled his eyes. "Come on, Jennifer. We're talking computers here. Film editing is a complex, technical process. You can't just walk in the door and pick it up. And for this project you're going to need an excellent visual sense to make smooth transitions from one sequence to the next."

David's gaze was more of an honest appraisal. "Who could have a better visual sense than an artist?"

"But that's not all," Philo protested. "She'd need an auditory sense. There's all the synchronization of sound."

"Wanda can do the technical stuff," David said. "Jennifer, you and I can do the creative."

"I get it," Philo said. "This is another way for you to spend more time together."

Jennifer grinned. "As Lionel, the erstwhile Sherlock Holmes, would say, elementary, my dear Philo."

IF JENNIFER HAD KNOWN what she was getting into, she might not have offered her help so rapidly. For four days she spent the daylight hours juggling her responsibilities at the shop. Her nights were consumed with staring at bits and pieces of videotape shown on four television screens in one of the editing rooms at Vids 'R' Us.

Once she got beyond her fear of the technology involved, Jennifer did enjoy the editing process. It was like making a mosaic or working in stained glass. She and David selected the tiny sparkling pieces and put them together to create a whole picture.

As Jennifer tried to balance the light values, integrate the transitions and match the narration, her concept of film was changing. Instead of enjoying the flow of the story unfurling, she saw a series of still photographs, each sliding into the next.

Her awe of movie magic was rapidly disappearing, and Jennifer regretted that loss of innocence. As she learned to recognize the structural framework, her fascination with the finished product diminished.

Likewise, in her relationship with David, there were more and more instances when their communication was on a strictly practical level.

For hours they would sit together in the same small editing studio—near enough to touch, but not touching. His words, though always polite and considerate, were not the husky whispering of lovemaking. More often he spoke to her as he would to Wanda or to Philo.

Most perplexing, she would watch him on the screen during those sequences when he'd accidentally stepped in front of the camera. With strange detachment she would observe him, studying his physique, his profile and the smooth grace of his movement. He was handsome on film, she thought. Without trying he exuded a masculinity that was appealing and sensual. She was aroused by him, even as she wondered whether the magic had evaporated from their relationship.

Jennifer tried not to think about it, but she couldn't help it. In the few hours left to her for sleep every night, she tossed and turned and worried.

As she staggered into the shop on the morning of the fifth day, Beth was waiting at the door. "Give me the key, Jennifer."

Without protest Jennifer handed over her keys. "What are you doing here?"

"I'm opening up. And I am going to run things for the next couple of days. Whether you want it or not, I am going to help out."

Instead of protesting, Jennifer was docile as she followed her friend into the shop. "Was this Philo's idea?"

"I promised not to tell," Beth said as she flipped the Closed—Come Again sign to We Are Open. "But I don't see why I shouldn't. It was David. He called me last night and asked me to relieve you so you'd go home and sleep."

"David did that?"

In Jennifer's nearly exhausted state, she could barely make sense of Beth's words. David's concern was sweet, but she knew immediately why he hadn't wanted Beth to mention it. She had to laugh. Finally, he'd learned that she didn't like to have him tampering with her schedule and making decisions for her. "This time," she said aloud, "I think I'll forgive him."

Beth crossed her arms beneath her breasts and regarded her sternly. "I have no idea what you're babbling about, but I don't want you to explain. Go home, Jennifer. Go to sleep."

"But I need to take care of a couple of things here."

"I have worked the shop before," Beth informed her. "And there's nothing that can't wait for a day."

"Agreed." Before she shuffled out the door, Jennifer gave her friend a hug. "Thanks, Beth. I don't know why I didn't call you myself."

Beth raised her hand to her lips and blasted the discordant five-note intro to the *Wasp Man* theme. "Because sometimes, my dear silver-winged friend, you try to act like a superheroine."

Jennifer nodded, waved and hurried out the door. Yawning at every stop sign, she returned home. Her feet were so heavy that she could barely drag herself up the steps. She literally staggered through the door, forced herself to change into a nightgown and collapsed on the bed.

And then...she was wide awake.

She closed her eyes and told herself to sleep, but her mind was racing. Her fingers itched for something to do. Her formerly limp body made contrary twitching motions under the covers. *Stay in the bed*, she ordered herself.

Her toes wiggled.

*I mean it*, she commanded. *Go to sleep.*

She flipped onto her stomach, then to her back. She drew her legs up in a fetal position. Still, she was wide awake.

When the telephone rang, her legs bolted from the bed bringing her to an unnecessary upright position to answer the bedside phone. "Hello?"

"It's not too late," the now familiar voice whispered. "You can still change it. Tell David. He must think of the future."

"How did you get this number?"

"I know you. I know it is within your power to change it. Let the past remain in silence."

Jennifer paused before replying. Until now she'd dismissed the caller as some kind of harmless crank. What if this whispering person had something to do with the accidental fire that destroyed the *Wasp Man* episodes of the past? "Tell me what you want," she said.

"You know. You must know."

"I'm not good with riddles. Is this about the film?"

"The film that should be."

"There was a fire," Jennifer said. "Did you know about the fire?"

The telephone went dead.

Jennifer called the studio, asked for David and waited on hold while someone went to fetch him. She would bet money that her whispering caller was the same person who had arranged the convenient accident to destroy the *Wasp Man* tapes. It was, after all, footage from the past, and the caller was very concerned about forgetting the past and moving into the future. What future? It made no sense to Jennifer.

Until this call she hadn't been frightened by the voice, but a possible connection with the accident gave her cause for alarm. A crank who sets fires can no longer be considered harmless.

As soon as David came on the phone, she blurted out, "I had another weird call."

"Beth told you, didn't she?" he interrupted.

"Yes, she did." Jennifer rushed to continue, "This time I was called here, at the house."

"I'm not trying to push you, Jen. But I really think you could use the sleep. Now why don't you unplug the telephone, pull the covers over your head and—"

"David!" she shouted. "I think my crank caller is the person who set the fire."

"What are you talking about?"

"Those weird phone calls I've been getting. The voice keeps talking about getting rid of the past. And that's just what the fire did. It wiped out the film from the past."

"Lock your doors, Jen. I'll be right there."

She stared at the telephone, which had gone dead in her hand. Lock the doors? She hung up the phone and chuckled. So David was dashing to her rescue. Apparently she wasn't the only one with a superhero complex.

Jennifer stretched and yawned. She definitely didn't feel like sleeping. Might as well make a fresh pot of coffee and meet David when he flew through the door, cape flapping in the wind.

He arrived in record time, pressed the doorbell and knocked.

"It's open," she shouted.

He stormed inside. "What do you mean, leaving your door unlocked when some anonymous nut has your home telephone number?"

"Coffee?" she offered.

"Black."

"Locking the door is no protection," she said. "There are twenty-four windows on the first floor of this house. I know because I have to wash them. And there are ten windows into the basement. If somebody wanted to get in here and attack me, a locked door wouldn't stop them."

"Dammit, Jen. I wish you hadn't told me that." He chose a seat on the wing chair opposite the sofa.

"Of course," she added, "there are also five telephones and the police patrol this area regularly."

"What's going on, Jennifer?"

"Sip your caffeine like a nice, fearless protector, and I'll explain."

She outlined her suspicions. For emphasis she repeated, "I've never felt threatened by the caller. He's never hinted that he would hurt me. In fact, he seems to be pleading."

"He? Is it a man?"

She considered for a moment. "Not necessarily. The voice is too husky to determine the gender. And there's always a kind of crackling static on the line."

"Then why did you refer to the voice as male?"

"Because I don't think a woman would be so strange."

She glanced over at him. For the first time since the accident, she saw the softening of his expression that came when they made love. Quickly he averted his gaze.

"David?" she said softly. "Is something wrong?"

"Wrong? Of course not. Why would you think something is wrong?"

"You haven't touched me, except to pat me on the back, in four days."

As was his habit when upset or confused, David bounced to his feet and began to pace. Jennifer watched him, reminded of their night together in the Brown Palace Hotel. "May I tell you a secret?" she asked.

"Of course you may." He fingered the antique shawl draped over her spinet. "Sure, tell me anything you'd like."

"Life would be a lot easier, David, if you would share your questions and emotions with me. Don't jump to conclusions. Just ask."

"How can I ask you for anything else?" His voice sounded tired, resigned. "Every time I turn around, you're helping me. I've felt like hell, watching you work day and night."

"It's been my choice."

"Can't you see that I'm taking advantage of you?"

"No, I can't," she said. "I thought this editing stuff would help me share in your career. It's a lot better than sitting home alone every night."

"Dammit, Jennifer, I want to do something for you."

"You don't have to do anything, David."

"Don't tell me that," he snapped loudly. His tension mounted. The pressure within him grew to unbearable proportions, a white-hot core of feeling that he forced himself to suppress. This rage, this fury, had to be contained. He clenched every muscle in his body, struggling to hold himself back. He feared an explosion. It would destroy everything, everything between him and the rest of the world. "I didn't mean to shout," he said.

"It's all right, David. Let it out."

"Don't patronize me, Jennifer. You don't know what it's like. You can't possibly know what I'm feeling."

"Why don't you tell me?"

"Give me a break. Give me a goddamn break."

He pivoted, turning away so that she couldn't see his struggle. His temples were pounding, throbbing. He tried to massage the tension away, but it grew more fierce.

"David," he heard her softly calling. "David, it's all right. You can tell me."

"Leave me alone, Jennifer. This isn't your fault."

"Nor is it your fault. You're in a pressure cooker, David. Anybody would feel it."

"No!"

His control was gone. He was too exhausted to contain it any longer. An adrenaline surge to his brain made everything sharp, painfully sharp. A gigantic weight pressed in on him. He drew back his fist. *Don't do it,* he commanded himself. *Control yourself.*

From the deepest recesses of his emotions he let out a shout, a primal yell of fury. His fist piled into the wall. He lashed out, again, deepening the dent he'd made in the wall above her piano. Again.

"Dammit, Jennifer. I can't take this anymore. Everybody wants something from me."

"It's all right, David."

"Don't give me that. It's not all right."

He saw her raising her hands, warding off his words. He didn't want to hurt her. "I love you, Jennifer, but right now I don't have anything left to give you. It's gone. I'm empty."

He closed his eyes and sank to the floor. He was breathing hard, sweating. Something inside him crumbled. The veneer of control that ruled his life had broken apart. He felt naked, exposed to her eyes.

"Look at me, David."

He responded. She was kneeling before him on the floor, looking concerned. Her cool white hand reached out and stroked his fevered flesh.

"I understand." Her voice sounded matter-of-fact, not condemning or accusing.

There were all these criteria and restrictions on their relationship. He had to be self-sufficient, successful. He had to be able to support her. In that moment he realized that all the restrictions were of his own making. "What if I fail, Jen?"

"I guess you'll have to start over."

"What will that mean for us?"

"I don't know. Real live relationships aren't like the movies."

"I guess I'm not much of a hero."

"You're human." She took his hands in hers. "And human beings get angry. And they make mistakes. You give so much to other people. Give something to yourself, David."

"I want to be better than that."

His tension had been spent. He felt utterly vulnerable, but not alone. He pulled her to him, needing the comfort she could give him.

For long minutes they sprawled together on the floor of her house. In silence.

When David began to speak, the words flowed in an uncensored rush from his unconscious. "When I was a kid, I wanted to grow up like Uncle Clayton. He was creative and powerful and strong. Not many kids have a real superhero in the family. I used to think that I was Wasp Man, that I had super strength hidden inside. And I hid a lot of other things. Wasp Man doesn't get angry. He's selfless and good. He rescues people. But I couldn't rescue my uncle. He didn't want me around anymore."

"He wasn't perfect, David."

"Maybe when he had the accident, he knew that." As he spoke, David knew he had finally discovered the truth. His uncle wasn't rejecting him. "He didn't want me to see him as an ordinary mortal. He didn't want me to know that he was an ordinary human, like everybody else. Superheroes don't exist except in the movies." He exhaled a deep breath. "What happens now, Jen? What if I fail?"

She nestled against him. "When I was younger, it wouldn't have mattered. I probably would have blithely said that love conquers all. And hoped for a happy ending. Now I know that happy endings have to be worked for."

"If I fail, is it over between us?"

"Of course not. David, I believe in you. Not Wasp Man."

He held her, drawing comfort and solace from her warmth. Strangely he felt his eyes beginning to sting, and he clung to her.

"If this project doesn't work," she murmured, "you'll find another."

"But I'll never find another you."

Her body felt so good to him. Safe, he was safe from the decision-making and the hassles and the budget overruns. There with Jennifer he could be himself. And that knowledge was liberating.

There were no special rules for a relationship, he realized. Only the two of them. And their needs. "I still want to make your life into something special," he said.

She brushed the hair off his forehead and kissed him. "You already have."

# 11

THAT NIGHT DAVID SHOWED her precisely how special she was to him. His caresses held a new tenderness. His kisses, always spectacular, urged her to new heights of passion. When they had fulfilled their desire, they slept in each other's arms, cradled in the renewed security of whole, mutual loving.

The next morning Jennifer shopped. She knew that the making of the Wasp Man epic was nearing completion and decided that gag gifts were in order for all the participants. In this instance, being a retailer was a definite advantage. Jennifer Watt, owner of Watt's Up, could truly let her fingers do the walking. After only three telephone calls she had purchased all the gifts at bargain wholesale prices. "Not bad," she congratulated herself. "And it's only ten o'clock."

She bounced into the bedroom and woke David. He glared at the clock and bolted from the bed. "Noon flight," he said, charging into the bathroom.

Humming contentedly, Jennifer meandered into the kitchen to fetch another cup of coffee. She'd already checked with Beth and arranged to take another day off. This day, she'd decided, was for her. To do with as she pleased.

And she wanted to spend her time with David. His outburst the day before made her feel closer to him than ever before. With the release of his pent-up anger they could truly share on the deepest level.

She was also ready to sketch and paint. Without questioning that urge she went into the spare bedroom. Ever since she'd moved into the house, she'd intended to convert this room into a studio. Though it was still a chaotic storage area, Jennifer knew exactly where her art supplies were buried. She dug out a portable easel, several sketchbooks, the watercolors and a handful of brushes.

Freshly showered and shaved, David burst into the room. "There you are," he said.

"Here I am."

He picked his way through the boxes and reached for her hand. Since both of her hands were full of potentially messy painting equipment, his romantic gesture was foiled. Instead of touching her, he flashed his gorgeous smile. "Come away with me. Let's fly to California on silver wing."

She looked out the window as she considered. It was a dismal gray day. Though the leaves on trees were a beautiful scarlet and yellow, there were dark clouds overhead, and the weather forecasters on the radio had been gleefully predicting an early snow. A trip to sunny California? It seemed a pleasant alternative.

David bombarded her with logical reasons why she should go. He didn't want to leave her alone with this weirdo who was making phone calls. She needed a break from the hectic routine at the shop. Beth had agreed to cover for her. There wasn't anything further they could do with editing the documentary until he returned with the *Wasp Man* footage. Lots of reasons.

But it wasn't until he spoke of the emotional reasons that she began to pack her bags. He wanted her to go. Their separations were difficult for him. He needed her.

To his surprise she was delighted to oblige.

She was teasing at the airport, animated on the plane, and when he rented a convertible, she leaned back in the fawn-colored bucket seat and basked in the warm California sunshine. As he parked in front of his uncle's Malibu Beach house, he couldn't help commenting, "What's gotten into you, Jen? I've never seen you so free and easy."

"Don't exactly know." She bounced from her seat and raced him to the trunk. "But I have a strong desire to slip into one of Uncle Clayton's all-purpose black bikinis and sun on the beach for the rest of day."

"Not much day left," he said. "It's almost five."

She looked up at the sky. The sun, though still beaming its warmth, was on the wane. It seemed impossible, but Jennifer had completely lost track of time. She was floating on a blissful continuum where there were no clocks, no responsibilities and no disruptions. "Tomorrow," she said. "Tomorrow I spend the day on the beach."

"And you'll wear one of the black bikinis?" he asked, slipping his arm around her waist.

"You bet. The skimpier, the better. I want a tan to take back to Colorado."

"You'll get no argument from me."

She snuggled in the circle of his arm and looked up at him with a mock innocent expression. "But what will we do tonight?"

"I have a dinner meeting. Come with me?"

"Okay...and after that?"

"Well, I need to make a few phone calls."

"And after that?"

He swept her into a close embrace. "I'll think of something," he murmured.

"I bet you will."

David barely made it through the dinner meeting with Uncle Clayton's attorney and his independent producer nephew, who volunteered to help David with his next documentary. David felt their firm handshakes, heard them speaking and tasted the nouvelle cuisine. But his attention was consumed with Jennifer. She was dazzling. Her laughter had never sounded so sweet, and she had never seemed so beautiful to him.

*This is what it's like,* David kept repeating to himself. *This is love.* Finally, he understood. This was the superlative feeling that caused lovers to leap, singers to croon and poets to rhyme. He felt as if he'd entered an enchanted atmosphere where every moment was heightened and every sensation was Jennifer.

That night, in the satin-sheeted bed beneath the skylight, they made love slowly and repeatedly. There was all the time in the world. The frantic pace of his life came to an utter standstill as he loved her, truly loved her. In her passion he found serenity. In her climax he found fulfillment.

The next morning Jennifer was uncharacteristically ready to be up and out of the house. By ten o'clock, after only one cup of coffee, she'd hustled David out onto the beach with towels and suntan lotion.

Lying on the beach beside her, he decided it was worth the rush. The black bikini—what there was of it—revealed far more than it covered, and he liked what he saw.

Her summer tan had already faded, but he could still discern a faint tan line. The high-cut bikini bottom showed an expanse of thigh that had apparently never been exposed to the sun. And the low-cut bikini top revealed a creamy-white half-moon at the top of each breast.

David was itching to massage suntan lotion into that delicate flesh. Jennifer stretched out on her back, arms above her head, and read his mind. "How about some lotion?" she said. "I don't want to burn."

He needed no further encouragement. After slathering coconut oil between his palms, he slowly caressed her. "It's a good thing there's nobody else nearby. Because I'd have to throw a blanket over you."

"Don't be silly, David."

"I mean it. This body is for my eyes only."

His suntan lotion massage was having an effect on her, and Jennifer forced herself to remain motionless. She closed her eyes, feeling the penetrating rays of the sun behind her eyelids.

Back in Denver the nip of autumn was in the air, but Malibu Beach was warm. Weather reports called it unseasonably warm, and Jennifer was glad. She could pretend the extra sunshine had been arranged especially for her.

As David's hands moved lightly along her calves to rub lotion round her knees, she suppressed a slight shudder. Maybe it wasn't just the sun that was making her feel hot. His fingers moved higher, encircling her thigh. Then higher. He lightly parted her legs, stroking the soft skin on the inside of her thigh.

"You need special attention here," he said. "I wouldn't want you to get a sunburn."

"Absolutely," she breathed.

When his fingertip slipped inside the bikini pants, she sprang to a sitting position. "David! This is a public beach."

"Nobody's around."

"Nonsense. Look there. Two kids—why aren't they in school?—playing in the water. And there, beyond the breakers, see the surfers. And a child with his grandmother, building a sand castle not more than fifty yards from us."

"Should we take a survey?" he murmured above the gentle wash of the surf on the sand. "Would they mind if I kissed you?"

"Let's don't ask."

She lay back and received his lips. The pressure of his mouth against hers was firm. He tasted salty, she thought, like a pure element. A force of nature.

When his tongue slipped through her lips, she lost the power of rational thought. Public beach or not, she slithered her arms around his neck. The lotion made her feel slick against him. And tender.

She broke away and jumped to her feet, not giving herself a chance to reconsider. If she stayed near him for one minute more, she would not be responsible for her actions. Jennifer charged down the sandy shore and plunged into the freezing waters of the Pacific.

He was right beside her. "Next best thing to a cold shower," he shouted. "By the way, can you swim?"

"Of course I can swim."

"I didn't know if they had water in Ohio," he teased.

"Cleveland, you geographic moron, is next to Lake Erie," she returned, diving over the breakers and beginning a strong crawl stroke.

David was beside her, surging through the waves like a crazed porpoise. She laughed at his clumsy splashing and got a mouthful of salty water. "Yuck. Oceans taste awful."

"Yeah? And what does yummy Lake Erie taste like?"

"Fresh water," she said as she sliced through the waves. Stroke, stroke, breath. She was a good swimmer, always had been. Despite the way her father had taught her to swim. Stroke, stroke, breath. He had taken her to the lake near their home when she was five. "Sink or swim," he'd said, throwing her off the pier.

Then he had sat and waited. Jennifer remembered the dark waters closing over her head. She hadn't been able to breathe. She was going to drown, she had known it. Sheer terror propelled her to the pier where her father had pulled her out, dripping and shivering.

"That's how life is, Jennifer," he'd said. "You got to jump right in and fight your way through it."

She had tried to believe him, but even as a child Jennifer hadn't wanted her life to be a continuous struggle through dim, murky waters. It didn't have to be. Why should it be?

## Seems Like Old Times    173

She'd taken swimming lessons. Stroke, stroke, breath. This was the way life should be, a smooth continuum of easy strokes through shimmering waves.

She turned back to see David, but he was right beside her. And she was amazed to see how little distance they had gone from where they'd entered the water. "Why aren't we farther along?"

"This is a big strong ocean, and you're swimming against the current."

"As usual," she said, taking a couple of breaths. That was precisely what her father would have said. *Still swimming against the current, Jennifer?*

They kicked toward the shore, catching a small wave and gliding on top of it. When Jennifer rose from the water, she had to rearrange the skimpy bikini, which apparently was never intended to enter the waves.

She rushed back to their beach towels and sprawled flat on her stomach, as much from modesty as from anything else. "This bathing suit is all stretched out of shape. David, the silly thing is falling off."

"Good old Uncle Wasp Man." He laughed. "I'm beginning to like the guy more and more."

"And I'm starting to believe those rumors that he used to flap around the beach wearing his silver cape and nothing else."

"It wouldn't surprise me." He eyed her long legs. "Time for more suntan lotion?"

"Why bother? You'd put the lotion on. I'd get hot and bothered. Then I'd remember this is a public beach. I'd jump in the water. And the suntan lotion would wash off."

"Sounds great to me."

"Obviously you've inherited more from your uncle than a terrific smile and dimples."

David sprawled on his beach towel. The warm sun felt good on his skin. This was the life he wanted for himself and Jennifer. No cares, no worries. He grimaced. What was he saying? At that very moment he could be hovering on the brink of financial disaster. Not true disaster, he corrected himself. Even if the documentary fell completely apart, David would not be destitute. Not when he had this house on prime Malibu Beach property to mortgage.

But it would be a long, long time before he was driving a Porsche. And he'd have to reevaluate his choice of career. That wouldn't take but a minute, he thought. David had tasted the excitement of working in a creative field, and he loved it. He was one beach bum who would never again be a banker.

He looked over at Jennifer. She would understand. She might not marry him, but she'd understand.

"David," she said lazily. "When this is all over, will you still want to move out here?"

"Would you move out here with me?"

She considered for a moment. "No."

"Then I'll have to be the Cecil B. deMille of Denver."

"No, again," she said. "I don't want you to hate me for holding you back."

David propped his head on one hand and studied the marvelous curve of her buttocks, the firm length of her legs. Even her feet were sculpted and beautiful. "Without you I'm not going anywhere."

"If you need to be here for your career, this is where you should be."

"Listen to me, you gorgeous hunk of female. I'll decide what's best for my career. I've got a lot to learn about movies and the work of a producer. Now it might be quicker to make contacts in Hollywood, but I've got a solid base of support

Denver. Waldheim, all my other banking connections, the gang at The Lodge in Conifer, Harriet Kelton. And you."

"Harriet?"

"The woman is rolling in dough, Jen. Remember? She owns The Lodge. And she wants to finance a feature film starring guess who."

Jennifer sat up to stare at him, then remembered the stretched bikini and flopped back down on her towel. "Are you going to do it?"

"I would in a minute if I had a decent script. There's a ready-made cast available at The Lodge." He cringed. "Can you imagine having to direct that circus in a full-length feature film?"

She shook her head and laughed, remembering David's struggle with them on the first day of taping.

"Of course," he said, "there is someone who has expressed an interest in directing."

"Philo?"

"Worse. Charlie Peyton, King of the Extras."

"Maybe Charlie wouldn't be such a bad director. He's certainly inventive." She considered a moment. "You know, David, Beth has a short story that she might be willing to adapt into a script."

"I don't want to hear about it. I've got to get through this documentary first."

"But you've already got the financing," she encouraged. "And Beth's story is set in Colorado. You could film right in Denver."

He pointedly changed the subject. "Great weather today, isn't it?"

Jennifer lowered her head onto her hands, thinking about Harriet and Charlie. "Does Harriet really have that much money?"

"Most of the people at The Lodge are fairly well off."

"You're kidding."

Nothing about these movie people was the way it seemed at first glance. She hadn't thought the gang from The Lodge was lacking funds, but she figured they needed cash, that opening a memorabilia section in her store was akin to charitable work. "I don't get it," she said. "If these people have money, why would they part with their treasured mementos?"

"I'm surprised at you, Jennifer. With your sharp perceptions about people, it should take you about three seconds to figure it out."

She closed her eyes, and the answer popped into her head. "Applause."

"Bingo."

They wanted to be remembered. If not for the parts they played, they wanted to be remembered as part of the golden era of their industry. It was awfully sweet when she thought about it that way. And harmonious with her feelings. She wanted to remember them—the way they were so many years ago *and* the way they were now. "What about you, David? Is applause the factor that motivates you?"

"A little," he admitted. "I'm looking forward to the time when the documentary is shown."

"What else?"

"Svengali," he said in one of his mysterious accents.

"Sven who?"

"There was a movie about him, I'm sure. He was a magician, a hypnotist, who transformed an average girl, Trilby, into a fabulous singer."

"Kind of like *My Fair Lady*?"

"Kind of. Anyway, I like the idea of manipulating everything into a state of perfection. A puppet master pulling the strings."

How did his statement apply to their relationship? Jennifer wondered. She wasn't aware of David pulling her strings, but that would be part of the magic, wouldn't it? "I'm not sure I like that picture," she said. "Are you manipulating me?"

"I've tried," he said with a laugh. "But you, my dear, are an adorably stubborn creature. Far too set in her ways."

They were quiet for a moment, letting their thoughts settle and allowing themselves to enjoy the pure physical pleasure of lying on a warm beach. David spoke first.

"You know, Jen, this Svengali tendency might be why other relationships haven't worked out for me in the past."

She buried her head in her arms. "I hate to hear about other relationships."

"This is important. An insight." He raised one finger in the air like a professor making a point to a reluctant class. "While I was a banker, there wasn't much chance for manipulating anything. I didn't have a lot of control. Sure, I could make recommendations, but the final decisions were always with groups. I guess I took out my manipulative urges on my relationships."

"You have no idea how blah that makes me feel," she said, half teasing and half serious. "I would much rather think that you were swept off your feet by my charm, wit and beauty. Not that our relationship is the happenstance of good timing."

They exchanged a glance. Ever since they'd met, they had been bemoaning the bad timing that kept them apart—his move to Malibu Beach and his embarking on a new career; her need to be closely involved in the operation of her shop rather than being a free-spirited artist who could go anywhere at any time.

Externals. All of those things were outside influences, Jennifer realized. The most important factor was that when she and David had met, they were both ready for a relationship. Their timing for love had been precisely right.

"Speaking of time," he said, "are you coming with me to those meetings this afternoon?"

"No, thanks. Last night was enough for me."

"Not going to let me pull your strings?" He reached over and ruffled her hair. "Come on, Jen. It might take all afternoon, and I don't want to be away from you that long."

"Wouldn't I be a distraction?" she teased. "Wouldn't I deter your brain from business?"

"You might be right about that."

"You go on, David. I want to lie here and enjoy the sun."

"That's what I mean by stubborn." He gave her a quick kiss and dashed toward the beach house.

An hour later, with the beginning pink of a sunburn coloring her skin, she wrapped herself in her towel and moved inside. She changed into a comfortable, flowing caftan and dug her painting equipment out of her suitcase. The luxury of having time to herself seemed decadent, and she decided to make the most of it.

The first time she'd seen the Malibu Beach house, she'd remarked on the upstairs office and the terrific skylights. In that room she set up a makeshift studio.

When David telephoned at five o'clock to ask her to join him and his associates for dinner, she cheerfully declined. "And don't you rush," she reassured him. "I'm having a wonderful time."

"What are you doing?"

"You'll see."

The spirit of Uncle Clayton must have been haunting her sketchbook because Jennifer had completed two vivid watercolor paintings of Wasp Man and a rough sketch of the suit of armor at the foot of the stairs. She was concentrating on a detailed head-and-shoulders portrait of Uncle Clayton, using a photo of him in his later years.

Perhaps, she thought as she studied the vibrant face beneath her brush strokes, Clayton Forbes was a good artist's subject because he'd spent much of his life in silence. As Wasp Man he was unable to speak. Then he had actually lost his golden voice. The impression he had created depended solely on the visual. If the boatloads of bikinis and women's bathrobes were any indication, his visual presentation had been excellent.

She wondered about his relationship with Harriet Kelton. In many of the interviews other people had been rather blatant in their suggestion that Clayton and Harriet were an item. Yet Harriet refuted it. The older woman would only say that she respected and admired Clayton's ability as an actor, but Jennifer had noticed a bitterness in her denials.

If there had been a relationship, Jennifer thought, it must have been hard on Harriet. After all, she had been a star first. She was in the running against Janet Gaynor for the first Academy Award for Best Actress. Then her career had faded. Harriet Kelton would be best remembered for her work in silent films.

More silence, Jennifer thought.

By the time David returned, she had completed five pictures: four of Clayton Forbes and one nude illustration of David himself.

She hurried down the stairs to meet him, wanting to keep her sketches a surprise. Flinging her arms around his neck, she greeted him with an enthusiastic kiss.

"Wow," he said, coming up for air. "Maybe I should leave you alone more often."

"No way, buster. Remember. You're going to be Denver's answer to movie moguldom. You and me, babe. Together forever."

She watched as his expression became guarded. "First, the good news," he said. "The contracts are signed. *Wasp Man Speaks* will be shown on two cable networks and most PBS stations."

Her excitement for him was tempered by the anticipation of the bad news that she felt sure was coming. "That's nice, David."

"Better than nice. It means that as long as the film is completed, I will not lose money. I'm not going to be wildly wealthy, but I will break even. If it's good and more stations pick it up, I'll do better."

"Wonderful." She gave him a hug. "I want to celebrate, David. But I have this nagging suspicion that you're going to tell me some bad news."

"I'm going to have to be spending some time out here. Maybe one week a month."

Jennifer swallowed hard. One week a month? That didn't sound too terrible. Lots of relationships survived long-distance separations that took up far more time. "Maybe that's positive," she said. "I'll appreciate you more when you're around."

"And I have to go on a promotional tour with *Wasp Man Speaks*." He lowered the boom. "It will probably take three to four weeks."

She thought he looked sheepish, but he didn't apologize. Why should he? If it was necessary to his career, he didn't have much choice. "Anything else? Any more little bombshells up your sleeve?"

"That's all." He gave a little shrug of his shoulders as if dismissing the unpleasant implications of his travel arrangements. "Now what were you doing this afternoon?"

"I'll show you."

As she led him up the stairs, she felt a chill inside, a fear that these trips were only the tip of the iceberg. Of course she realized that it was necessary for his career—especially now in its embryonic stage—that he be free to go where he was needed. Still, the prospect was daunting.

Somehow she'd formed the mental image of a committed relationship. And it included two people, together. Like her parents. She gasped and shuddered.

"Are you cold?" David asked.

"A bit," she replied. But the icy fingers that tore at her heart had nothing to do with the temperature. Her parents? That wasn't the relationship she wanted. Though they'd never complained, Jennifer had always known that her mother and father were living in a prison of their own making. Their relationship, her family, represented a confinement. No, she didn't want that.

But she didn't want to be always waiting for David's return. She needed to be with him. And he wanted to be with her. He'd said so on the beach only a few hours ago.

Externals, she reminded herself. There were reasons beyond them that condemned them to a long-distance relationship. Damn. Why couldn't he have stayed a banker?

She flicked the light switch upstairs and displayed her afternoon's endeavor. The pictures were ranged around the room, and David studied each as if he were in an art gallery. "These are good, Jennifer. I mean, these are really good."

When he came to the nude study, David paused. He was facing away from her, and she could see the tensing of his shoulders. "Don't you like it?" she asked.

When he turned to face her, she saw a reflection of his new vulnerability in his smoky-gray eyes. It was the look she had captured in her watercolor. Her artistic skill allowed her to create a portrait of a man. Her talent gave the picture depth. She'd painted the eyes of a man in love.

Without a word he came to her and embraced her.

"Oh, David." She sighed. "I wish we never had to be apart."

In the gentle shelter of his arms Jennifer came very close to wishing that the Wasp Man documentary would be destroyed, that it would be a huge flop.

# 12

BY MONDAY MORNING the weather in Denver had cleared. The tang of autumn was in the air, invigorating and as crisp as the first bite of a red October apple. Jennifer's mood had been lightened by a weekend of lovemaking, but her doubts about the feasibility of a long-distance relationship had not been erased.

Uncharacteristically she awakened early, showered, dressed and hurried to check in at Watt's Up. It was almost as if she needed to reassure herself that her shop had not disappeared over the weekend. A short drive, and she was there. The cheery, hand-painted sign still hung above the doorway. The window display was neat and intriguing. Jennifer swung around the back to park. As she unlocked the rear entrance, she smiled. Watt's Up. At least there was some stability in her life.

She was inspecting the movie memorabilia, deciding which items to display, when Beth entered. "You're back," Beth said. "And you have a tan. Tell me all about your glamorous weekend in Lotusland."

"Oh, the usual—" Jennifer feigned boredom "—hobnobbing with Shirley MacLaine and George Hamilton, dining at Ma Maison, shopping on Rodeo Drive."

"Not really?"

"Actually, I never left the house," Jennifer said. "But all in all, it was pretty spectacular."

"What else?"

"Surely you don't want all the lurid details of what happened in the late Wasp Man's boudoir."

"Stop!" David shouted as he bounded through the door. "It's a little early for a kiss-and-tell biography."

"Early in the morning?" Jennifer asked. "Or early in the relationship?"

"Both." He kissed her lightly on the lips.

"You mean it's going to get even more depraved?" she teased, gleefully rubbing her hands together. "Oh, goody. I can't wait."

"This woman should not be turned loose on the world until after twelve o'clock noon," he said. "Hi, Beth."

"Hi, yourself." She turned to Jennifer. "Are you going to need my help today?"

"If you can stay, I can use you. I really need to rearrange the inventory. Let me find out what this wayward movie mogul is up to, and then we'll get started."

She turned to David. Though her manner was brisk and businesslike, Jennifer felt a surge of warmth simply because he was near her. He looked marvelous in the morning, she thought, but no more so than late at night.

As he talked, a remembered picture of David, reclining on the pale satin sheets on the bed in Malibu Beach, formed in her mind. With an artist's appreciation for his masculine physique she imagined the play of shadow and light across his chest, the sinews of his biceps, the shaded hollow at the base of his throat. She leaned back against the counter and enjoyed the memory, not hearing a word he said.

"Any suggestions?" he asked. "Any ideas?"

"I'm sorry," she said. "Could you repeat that?"

"Jennifer, where's your brain today?"

With a wicked grin she whispered, "Malibu…midnight on Saturday…champagne-colored satin sheets…"

"Enough. I remember."

Though his roguish smile was in place, David was actually blushing. Jennifer chuckled. That should pay him back for embarrassing her on a public beach. They really were well suited to each other, she thought, a couple of blushing old fogies. "Now, David, what were you saying?"

"In a nutshell," he said with an exasperated sigh, "I dropped off the *Wasp Man* tapes to Wanda this morning, and she thinks we'll have a completed film on Friday."

Jennifer gestured to Beth, who had been trying to fade into the woodwork while the two of them talked. "Did you hear that? We might actually be able to spend time with our men. Without interference from Wasp Man."

Both women applauded.

"Thank you." David bowed. "Here's the problem. There are four executive types coming out from Hollywood on Friday, and they want to see the film. Do you two ladies have any ideas where we could show this epic?"

Jennifer and Beth pondered for a moment. They mentioned several possibilities and discarded each one. Then inspiration struck. "Delilah's," Jennifer said.

"Perfect," Beth concurred.

David looked at them as though they'd lost their minds. "Delilah? The artist who specializes in neon tongues?"

"Her house is a mansion," Jennifer assured him. "It's huge, and she has a huge room with a giant television screen."

"Do I dare ask why Delilah has a giant TV?"

"It's not really too kinky," Beth said. "In fact, it's a common malady that occurs in Denver every autumn. Bronco fever. Delilah is a fanatic football fan."

"Are we talking about the same woman?"

"Absolutely," Jennifer said. Thoughtfully she added, "But I'm not sure that it's the football game that keeps Delilah interested. Rumor has it that she's trying to get John Elway, the quarterback, to pose nude."

"What a party that could be," Beth said, and she listed the possible guests. "The artists, the gang from The Lodge, everybody who worked on the film, your movie executives."

"All those people?" David asked doubtfully.

"A premiere," Jennifer announced. "The Grand Premiere Showing of *Wasp Man Speaks*. I'll call Delilah."

David paced a few steps and gave her one of his raised-eyebrow looks. "Maybe we should give this a bit more thought."

"Nonsense." Jennifer picked up the telephone. "Her house is perfect, and Delilah will love it."

Jennifer was right. Delilah was gracious and very happy to play hostess. Her home was opulent, and she thoroughly enjoyed throwing parties.

During the next four days the party plans progressed without a hitch. Jennifer and Beth kept busy with reorganizing inventory space and hanging Halloween costumes.

On Thursday afternoon David informed Jennifer that the edited master print was being run. Jennifer informed Beth.

"Yay," Beth said weakly as she gave up trying to fit a square foot of boxes into a half foot of shelf space. "Jennifer, I hate to point out the obvious, but you need more room."

"You're right. The toy store on my left is moving to another location, and they asked if I'd like to lease their space. I could put a door right here and connect the stores."

"Do it," Beth advised.

"I don't know if I can afford to."

"What if you had a partner? I could stick my print shop in the corner, and we'd both get what we need."

They exchanged a grin. "Let's do it," Jennifer said.

"But not in the next ten minutes, okay?"

Together they said, "Break time."

## Seems Like Old Times

They plunked down in two antique, decoupage rocking chairs near the front window display. The store was blissfully quiet.

"What a week!" Jennifer said, stretching and yawning.

"Incredible," Beth agreed as she rocked. "But this premiere party is going to be worth it."

"And the film is finished."

Jennifer sank into her own thoughts. Happy as she was to have the documentary completed, there was also a twinge of regret. David would go on the road to promote the film. He'd be back and forth to Los Angeles. Then there would be another project.

"What's up?" Beth asked. "You have that look."

There was no point in trying to cover up. Beth knew her too well. "I just don't know how long this is going to last."

"You and David?"

She nodded. "He's got the final distribution agreements, but he has to take a month-long promotional tour."

"For a documentary?"

"The way he explained it, *Wasp Man Speaks* is going to be the first in a series. David needs to make sure that all the PBS stations that pick it up are absolutely thrilled with it so they'll take the next one, and the next after that."

Beth cocked her head to one side. "So? What's the problem?"

"After the tour he's committed to be in California for one week a month. I'm scared. I don't want to tie him down, but if he's gone all the time, what kind of relationship can we have?"

"I've gotten a taste of what it's like," Beth commiserated. "With all the work Philo has been doing on *Wasp Man Speaks*."

"At least Philo is done every night at five o'clock. He has to be. David can't afford overtime."

"Oh, no, you're wrong, Jennifer. He's been staying out regularly until after midnight?"

"Keeping up with his other projects?"

"He has no other projects right now."

Beth turned pale, and Jennifer wished she could call back her unwitting indiscretion. "Of course, there's some over time," she amended. "And I haven't been around for a couple of days."

"For the past two weeks," Beth stammered, "He...he hasn't come home until late. Really late."

"Beth, I'm sorry." Jennifer had never seen her friend so devastated. She'd never known Beth without Philo. And in all the time they had been friends, Jennifer had never heard either of them complain about the other. Sure, they had disagreements, but nothing serious. The two went together like salt and pepper. Abbott and Costello. Laurel and Hardy. It had never occurred to Jennifer that their relationship could be in trouble. "Have you been having problems?"

"Not until now."

"Then don't take my word for it. Maybe David and Philo have an arrangement I don't know about."

"It's not only what you said, Jennifer. He's been acting strangely. Philo has always told me everything—more than I wanted to know. But lately he's been secretive."

"I'm sure there's a simple explanation."

"You're probably right." Beth straightened her shoulders. "Are you going to be seeing David tonight?"

"I'm supposed to meet him at the studio at five o'clock. For a preview showing of the finished print."

"Five o'clock? I think I'll go with you."

Jennifer started to speak, to offer words of comfort, but she stopped herself. Her friend's attitude told her that consolation would not be appreciated.

Jennifer had never seen sweet, demure Beth look so determined. The gentle curve of her brow had lowered into a scowl. Her usual smile had constricted to a tense line. If Philo had been messing around, Jennifer didn't envy him.

After the swamp monsters had returned from the Sixteenth Street Mall, where they'd been promoting the Halloween costumes, and Jennifer's evening clerk had arrived, she departed with Beth, who scrunched down on her side of the van like a little black cloud. Jennifer tried to ease her friend's anger. "Beth, I might have been mistaken. I don't want to start any kind of trouble between you and Philo."

"It's not your fault."

"Then why do I feel so guilty?"

"Because, Jennifer, you're always trying to please everybody—me, David, Philo, Harriet, your parents and the world at large. I'm sorry if this sounds harsh, but this is one time you can't make me feel better."

"Me? Trying to please everybody?"

"I don't want to talk about it, Jennifer. Please."

She respected her friend's wishes but pondered her statement. Jennifer wasn't aware of any striving to please. In fact, she made conscious efforts to set out boundaries. Hadn't she stuck to her guns until David learned not to make appointments for her?

Still, she hadn't told David how upset she was about his travel schedule. And, she thought with some chagrin, she had readily placed his needs before hers by assuming that travel was necessary for his career.

She pulled up at the rear entrance to the studio and dropped Beth off before she went to park the van.

Before she had locked the van doors, she saw Beth and Philo leaving together. Philo plucked nervously at his beard, and his wife was flushed with radiant anger.

Jennifer didn't bother to wave to them. They were s[o] caught up in their separate world that they would not hav[e] noticed. Instead, she ducked inside to find David.

He was on the telephone, verifying with the visiting e[x]ecutives that they would be in town the next night for th[e] premiere showing of *Wasp Man Speaks*. When he hung u[p] the phone and turned to her, she could see palpable reli[ef] spreading across his features. "Jennifer, I'm so glad to se[e] you."

He pulled her into an embrace and just stood there, hol[d]ing her. His hug felt tired, and his head was heavy on he[r] shoulder. Poor David, she thought. The stress and strain [of] this final few days of preparation had taken their toll on hi[m]. She wanted to nurture him, to feed her own strength into him[.]

But what about her own needs? Perhaps this would be [a] good time to speak up and ask about his schedule—a pr[o]pitious time to tell him how she would miss him, how muc[h] she wanted a commitment.

As she gazed into his eyes, he looked so terribly tired. Sh[e] couldn't add to his burden. Not now. "Are you sure you wan[t] to show me this print?" she asked. "You look like what yo[u] need is a good night's sleep."

"I want your opinion, Jennifer. I'm too close to the proje[ct] to be objective, and I want to be prepared for the criticism I'[ll] get from those Hollywood guys tomorrow night."

"But I'm not a film critic," she objected.

"You know more than you realize, Jen." He gave her a la[st] little squeeze and took her hand. "Follow me, madam."

As he led her downstairs and along a corridor, she notice[d] a shuffle in his usually vigorous step. "You must be e[x]hausted," she said. "I've never seen you pass up an oppo[r]tunity for a movie line before."

"What line is that?"

"The line from all those dreadful old horror movies." She dropped his hand, limped down the hall in a foot-dragging Igor impersonation and lisped, "Walk this way."

Her joking produced a small chuckle from David, and she bounced back to an erect posture. "Why don't we take the videotape to my house and watch it? Then it can be *Bedtime for Bonzo*."

"Because, Jennifer, this is a one-inch broadcast quality videotape. It won't fit your VCR."

He unlocked the door to a fairly large screening room that was separate from the other areas he had rented. There were several folding chairs, lots of crates and boxes, five director's chairs, a VCR and a forty-eight-inch television screen.

"Charming place," Jennifer commented dryly.

"Vids is a working studio, not intended for grand premieres," he said. "Everything is functional. This area, however, needs work."

"I can tell."

Though the walls were wainscoted with white acoustical tiles, the room seemed like a perfectly awful place to show films. It was basement level, with three high windows on each of two walls, and a steel exit door with a horizontal push bar.

"Isn't there a lot of street noise?" she asked.

"Some," he agreed as he went around the room, closing the particularly ugly orange curtains on the windows.

She gestured to the five director's chairs that seemed to be set up for an audience. "Is someone joining us?"

"No, those were for earlier. We've already shown the print three times. Harriet and Charlie Peyton have seen it. And the guys who own this building."

"And what did they all think?"

"It was mixed. Charlie loved it, but Harriet seemed to be reserved. Wanda the film editor thinks it's a masterwork."

He ejected the videotape and checked the cassette to make sure it had been rewound after the last showing. Then he went to the corridor door and locked it.

Jennifer noticed this precaution. "Have you had any more accidents? Like the fire?"

"Not a thing. And in case you're wondering, this isn't the only copy of the film. Philo has one. Wanda has one. And there are two more videocassettes in a bank vault downtown."

"That's impressive security," she said.

"Please take your seat, madam. It's show time."

While Jennifer got comfortable in one of the director's chairs facing the screen, David turned off the glaring overhead lights, started the VCR and sat in the chair beside her.

"The beginning credits," he whispered, "are a surprise."

As the *Wasp Man* trumpet blared and the voice of the original TV series announcer intoned the melodramatic intro, opening credits ran. They were superimposed over the paintings of Clayton Forbes that Jennifer had done during their last weekend in Malibu.

"David," she gasped. She stared at him in the darkness, seeing the gleam of his smile. Then she turned back to the screen. Her paintings. They were beautiful. The colors were vibrant. Brushwork was not evident on the screen, but the form showed brilliant liveliness. "Run it again," she demanded.

He laughed and went to the VCR, rewinding and showing the beginning of the documentary again. It wasn't until the fourth time through that Jennifer noticed her name: Opening Credits by Jennifer Watt.

She was speechless. Not only was she gratified to see the skill and talent evident in her artwork, but she also knew that the wide exposure of television would bring her some recognition. She was committed. She was an artist.

As he rewound the tape for a fifth showing, she left the director's chair and went to him. "Thank you, David."

"I'm glad you like it. For a minute there I thought you were going to give me a lecture about using your work without your permission."

"I probably would have refused," she admitted. "I probably would have told you that there were other artists who did better work. But it is good, isn't it?"

"Did you ever doubt it?"

"Oh, yes," she said. "Constantly."

She stepped into his embrace, cleaving to him. While the documentary continued, unwatched, David kissed her, and she felt an unbelievable surge of power and strength that seemed to come from beyond her. Tension coiled her muscles, and yet she was light, weightless.

His body was warm as she pressed herself against him, reveling in the special excitement they shared. They fit together so well. Her softness complemented his hard, sinewy body, and his kisses always made her feel as if she were floating through star-filled eternity.

She drew her lips away from his. A blissful sigh puffed through her parted lips, and she opened her eyes.

There had been obstacles—the physical separations, the intense pressure of a career change, the exhausting work of filmmaking, the accident, the whispery phone calls. And still she could gaze into his eyes in the darkness and say, "David, I love you."

"And I love you, Jenny mine."

"I know you're tired, darling."

"I'll live," he said.

"Let's watch the film quickly and then...home to bed."

He spun the cassette back to the beginning. They sat beside each other, holding hands.

Five minutes into the documentary Jennifer was thoroughly absorbed. She'd seen every film clip used, but when they ran together in an edited piece, the magic returned. She was caught up in the life of Clayton Forbes. Harriet Kelton turned back into the fascinating creature whom Jennifer so admired in her early motion pictures. They all looked and sounded marvelous. She giggled when one of the swamp monsters gave a thumbs-up sign to the camera.

"David, this is wonderful."

She squeezed his hand, but he didn't squeeze back. She glanced over to see his head slumped against his chest. He jerked awake, turned to her and smiled. "What do you think?"

"There's about half an hour to go."

He rose, stretched and widened his eyes. "I can't sit in a dark room," he said. "I'll go get a pizza and be right back."

"Okay. Hurry."

As he staggered toward the exit, she heard him stumble over one of the boxes, curse and push his way outside. A whoosh of fresh October air swept over her as the door closed by itself and locked.

Jennifer went to the VCR and rewound the tape to see the part she'd just missed. If David wanted a critique, she wanted to be able to swear that she'd loved every minute of the film.

By the time Harriet Kelton carefully pronounced the last voice-over while Clayton Forbes stood proud and heroic in his Wasp Man cloak, Jennifer was enthralled. To be sure, it wasn't perfect. There were a few minutes when her mind had wandered, but overall she thought the documentary was a fair and accurate portrait of a man who had plied the craft of acting in several different arenas and had contributed to and learned from each.

She went to the VCR and rewound the film, thinking that she might sneak a peek at her opening credits again. Then she heard it. A whisper. "Jennifer."

"What?" She spun around. There was no one there, but the jumble of boxes had taken on a more threatening aspect.

She ran to the light switch and flicked it on. Jennifer stood very still, blinking in the glare and telling herself that she was hearing things. No one else was in the room. It was impossible for anyone else to be in the room. David had locked the door.

The videocassette was still rewinding, making a faint, rattling whir. That must be it, she thought with a shrug. Her ears had been playing tricks on her. The whispering sound must have come from the VCR.

The rewind finished, and Jennifer turned the machine off. The silence in the screening room was ominously thick. Though she'd decided there had been no whispering, Jennifer found herself straining to listen. She jumped when she heard the rasping voice. "Jennifer, please help me. I have something important to tell you."

"What do you want?"

She looked around the room, unable to discern where the voice was coming from.

"Jennifer. Jennifer. We must plan for the future."

It was coming from outside. She looked at the unevenly closed curtains at each of the windows. The whisperer was probably leaning down in the window well, staring in at her.

She had three choices: stand there like an idiot; leave through the corridor; or go outside and confront the whisperer.

"Jennifer," came the whisper. "Don't be afraid. I won't hurt you."

She'd seen enough suspense movies to know that "I won't hurt you" was usually what the ax murderer said before hacking his victims. There was no way she'd fall for that line. "I've had enough!" she said. "I don't know what you want, and I don't care."

She spun on her heel and went to the door that led into the corridor. She defiantly flung the door open. In the dimly lit hallway she saw the figure of a man. Jennifer screamed.

David dropped the pizza box and ran to her. "What is it?"

"David, thank God you're here." She grabbed his arm and dragged him through the screening room. "Come on."

"Jennifer, what the hell is going on?"

"Don't talk, just come with me."

She propelled him through the room and out the door. She ran up the concrete stairs from the basement exit. It was dusk, the time of day when shadows make hazy villains from waving branches and shrubs. In the area she thought was right outside the basement screening room, Jennifer halted and compelled David to stand still beside her. "We're here," she said. "We want to help you. Where are you?"

David glared at her. "What the hell are you doing?"

"The whisperer is out here," Jennifer said as she scanned the area. "I heard the voice."

"Right, Jen. Listen, the pizza is getting cold, and I'm not awake enough to play any games."

She held up her hand for silence, and they listened to the whistle of wind through the trees. Then came the voice. "Jennifer. Jennifer. Please listen to me."

David went into a crouch. He pointed toward the corner of the building and held a finger to his lips for silence. As he crept forward, Jennifer followed.

"Jennifer," the whisper said again. "You understand me. You know we can't stay in the past."

David approached a thick evergreen shrub that stood beside one of the window wells. He motioned for Jennifer to go around to the other side.

## Seems Like Old Times          197

"Now, Jen!" At his shout they charged around the bush and ran smack into each other. On the ground between them was a cheap cassette tape recorder. It whispered, "Jennifer. Jennifer. Please listen to me."

She picked it up and turned the switch to Off. Then she looked at David. "Why?"

"Apparently they wanted to lure you outside."

"Oh my God, David. The tape! Somebody is going to steal the tape." She dashed to the basement doorway and hammered on the steel door. Turning back to David, she said, "We've got to break a window. They're probably in there right now."

"Why don't we go around to the front and use my key?"

She winced as she remembered, "You have copies."

"Right." He took her by the arm and directed her around the building. "It's cruel and it's stupid. But I think this is just a prank, Jen."

"Don't patronize me." She jerked away from him. "Not until we see whether there's been another 'accident.'"

They went the circuitous route to the front of the building and returned to the screening room. Everything was exactly as it had been before. "You see," he said. "Lucky for you there's nothing wrong."

"What is that supposed to mean?"

"You were the one who dragged me out the door without a moment's explanation." He unloaded the film from the VCR. "Honestly, Jennifer. You spacy artist types are all alike. No foresight."

She gritted her teeth, forcing herself not to say anything. How could he be so insensitive? He knew she was struggling with the dichotomy of being a free-spirited artist and a responsible retailer.

And why did she remain silent? Silent like Clayton Forbes. Silent like Harriet Kelton. Why couldn't she speak? It was important for her to tell him what she needed.

She recalled Beth's statement. Was she trying to please David at her own expense? Her words spilled out in a tumble. "I know you're tired, David. But there is no excuse for a comment like that."

"I was teasing," he protested.

"It wasn't my fault that I dragged you out the door," she said. "I was frightened, and you weren't here. As usual."

"What are you implying, Jennifer?"

"Why don't you try sticking around long enough to find out?"

She could feel her frustration fueling itself, building its own head of steam until it became an unstoppable force within her. *Don't*, she told herself. *He's only teasing*.

Yet her anger would not be quenched. She couldn't count on him. Why had he arranged to spend all that time in Hollywood? How could he agree to a promotional tour that would separate them for a month? He showed so little consideration for her fears and her feelings. And that hurt.

"Maybe we can talk about this later," David said. "After you've calmed down."

"Of course you'd say that. Later. With you, David, it's always later."

She paused, shocked by her bitchy tone but unable to stop herself. The unpremeditated words seemed to be flowing of their own accord. "I want a commitment from you, David. A real relationship. I need for you to be with me, and I hate when you take off on these damn trips. I'm tired of waiting."

"It won't be much longer, Jennifer," he placated.

"Either forget that promotional tour, David. Or forget us."

He picked up the film cassette and held the door open for her. "I'll take you home."

Home? The house she'd bought no longer seemed like home to her. Home included David, but the chill in his words made her feel as if the door to that place had been closed and locked.

## 13

THEY DROVE to her house in separate cars. David used the beat-up Ford Escort he'd purchased for five hundred dollars through an ad in the newspaper, and Jennifer bumped along in her van. More than once she'd caught herself almost cruising through a stoplight, and somewhere along the route she'd lost track of David's car in her rearview mirror.

She found a parking place on the street opposite her house and fumbled up to the door in the dark. It would serve her right if he didn't even show up. The poor man was exhausted. The last thing he'd needed tonight was a nasty outburst from her.

She unlocked the door and tripped inside, wondering if she'd ever see him again. Of course she would. There was no way on earth she could avoid the grand premiere at Delilah's house.

Peeking through the front window, she watched for his car. Nothing. Five minutes passed. He wasn't coming. And it was all her fault. She'd delivered the brave ultimatum: Choose between your career and me. Apparently he had made his choice, and she would be spending the night alone.

Damn. With halting steps she went into the bathroom. Maybe she should check her reflection in the mirror to make sure she still existed. The face that stared back at her looked sad and tired. She ran hot water in the sink.

What next? Where did she go from here? Jennifer splashed water on her face. Start all over again? But there were so many starting points to choose from. She might elect to be the free and easy artist. David had given her new confidence in her ability. In spite of her anguish, she smiled at the remembrance of her paintings beneath the opening titles of the documentary. Those watercolor sketches had been good. She couldn't deny it.

She splashed another scoop of warm water on her face. Maybe the best place to start over was a rededication to her shop. With the addition of the movie memorabilia section she was doing more business than ever before.

*Concentrate on that*, she told herself, *become a successful retailer. Open a franchise. Create a chain of boutique art, movie and craft stores crisscrossing the nation.* Her mind painted a sorry picture of Joan Crawford in broad-shouldered, manfully tailored suits, striding through cold, loveless boardrooms.

Or perhaps she should return to the very beginning, her roots. She soaked a washcloth in steaming hot water and applied it to her face. If she went all the way back to childhood, she might be able to relive her life properly.

The warmth seeped through the cloth, soothing her. Roots? Every time she thought of her parents and the place she'd once called home, she was overcome with guilt. She could never do anything right for them, could never please them.

It wasn't only them. Mom and Dad represented a lot of other people—teachers, friends, associates. All those little voices lived within Jennifer. She couldn't please them. And she wouldn't accept their guilt.

She peeled the washcloth away from her face and looked at her reflection in the steamy mirror above the sink. "I can't do it anymore. I won't do it."

A heavy sob choked through her. "I have to please myself."

Jennifer sank down on the edge of the bathtub. No matter what they wanted, no matter what David wanted, she had be herself. Years of grieving flowed from her as tears streaked down her cheeks.

Then she heard the doorbell. David? She tried to stop crying, but the attempt was futile. Draping a towel around her shoulders, she went to answer the door.

The light in the foyer was dim, she thought. Maybe he wouldn't notice. She unlocked the door and quickly turned away from him.

David followed her into the room. "The pizza is cold."

"I'm not hungry, anyway."

Her tears wouldn't stop. Her shoulders heaved. Dammit, she didn't want to be crying. But, sometimes, sadness was a part of her, too.

She paced away from him, fearful that if he touched her, she would dissolve. With an effort she spoke through her tears. "I haven't been completely honest with you. Or with anybody. I've been trying so hard to be what I thought you wanted that I lost track of myself."

She faced him, aware that she must look like hell, but needing for him to accept her, anyway. "I meant what I said about needing a real relationship with you. I've pretended that I could continue without a commitment, but I can't. I don't want you to travel all the time. I don't want to be separated from you."

She couldn't look into his eyes. She was afraid of what she might see there, fearful that he was going to say goodbye. Gently he pulled her close. "I love you, Jen."

She laid her head on his shoulder. His nearness was so good, so kind. She could no longer pretend at restraint. Her body convulsed, and she wept.

Everything was fading. Through her sobs she had a vague sensation of being carried like a child into the bedroom. She could feel him loosening her clothing. Then he lay beside her, offering his strength. Nestled against him, she sniffled. "Thank you, David. For being here."

With her final tears she sensed a relief. Finally, she was free. She'd shown him this tragic, grieving part of her. And he hadn't fled. He'd accepted her. She snuggled against him. There was something important she needed to do, but she was incapable of action. Her tears subsided into sleep.

He stroked her hair, untangling the fine strands of honey gold, and the touch of it soothed him. His entire body throbbed with exhaustion, and he didn't entirely understand why she was so upset. Surely she couldn't believe that he would ever wish to leave her.

His eyelids drooped closed. He wanted to think about her, about their relationship. He wanted to make sense of everything. But not tonight. His head was too muddled. Softly he murmured, "Jennifer, I will always love you. We'll find the answers."

David drifted into a deep, unconscious sleep.

His dreams took him on a journey. He knew he had to get home, but the path was a steep, winding road between two towering, snow-covered mountain peaks. As he walked, his feet became mired in a sticky tar. Every step was an effort.

Then he saw Jennifer. She called to him in a melodic whisper, "Don't walk on the beaten path."

What a simple solution! He stepped to the side of the road and felt soft, billowing grasses beneath his feet. He moved swiftly along the road, running through sweet scented primroses. He was almost there, almost home.

Then he awoke. The first light of dawn was visible, creeping around the dark shades in her bedroom. It was morning, Friday morning. Tonight the executives from Hollywood would decide the fate of the documentary. He ought to be anxious, but David felt more comfortable with himself than he had in years.

He gazed at Jennifer, who lay spread-eagled, her slender body taking up three-quarters of the bed while he was crunched in a corner. He rearranged her to make more room for himself. Room in her life, he thought.

His future was more clear to him than it had been in a long, long time. It was time for him to do as he wanted. He might not be as rich as a prince. Nor as dashing as a sheik. Nor as constant as the sunrise. But he wanted this woman. If she would accept him, he meant to claim her for his own.

And what if he wasn't enough? All along he'd had the idea that she cared for him but that she demanded more from a marital partner. Before last night he'd thought it was the financial instability of his new career that disturbed her. Now he clearly saw that it was a matter of commitment.

She'd spoken her mind and told him that she didn't want him traveling so much. The travel was inescapable, however; it was part of his career. Would he have to choose between commitment to his career and commitment to his love?

He gazed over at her slumbering body. Cut her from his life? He would rather sever an arm.

He kissed the top of her head, and she stirred slightly. "Not morning," she mumbled.

"Afraid so, Jen."

She threw an arm across his chest, then jolted awake. Her slightly puffy eyes were wide and staring. She caressed his cheek and trailed her hand along the column of his throat. "Thank God, you're here. I thought I'd dreamed you."

In the warmth of her morning bed she stretched and yawned like a cat. Her movements against his body were frankly sensual, and David responded, turning his body to meet hers. If she rejected him and the relationship he could offer, this might be the last time they made love.

He felt a tremendous emptiness within him. A chasm that only she could fill.

They peeled away the odd bits of clothing they'd slept in and lay together, flesh against flesh.

Jennifer touched the scratchy stubble on his chin. It felt rough and prickly. Not like the springy hair on his chest. What a wonderful creature a man is, she marveled. So utterly different from herself. And this man, she thought, was the right man, the only man, for her.

With a painful jolt she remembered the circumstances. Her ultimatum. This man might be leaving her life. They might not settle their differences. There might not be a future for them.

As his strong hand skillfully caressed her torso, she willed away her fears and accepted the moment. This might be the last time she would share the incredible physical pleasure he was capable of arousing.

Her body hummed with feelings that she couldn't explain. Sharp sensations prickled along her skin and permeated her flesh. She explored his body, his magnificent body, memorizing and adoring his rugged hardness, and she molded herself against him.

He turned her to her back on the bed, and his loving touch discovered the secret crevasses of her desire. In a flashing montage she remembered. His suntan lotion caresses on the beach. The sensual feel of satin sheets in the Malibu Beach house. David's nervousness the first time at the Brown Palace Hotel. Making love on the sofa. And the rain. She remembered the torrential rainfall the first night they'd met.

That rain had washed her clean, changed her forever. Though her thoughts were of cool, drenching rain, her body was warm. Hot. She arched against him, drawing him close, opening her thighs and welcoming him.

His tantalizingly slow strokes throbbed within her, and she thrust her pelvis in a swifter rhythm. Their breaths came rapidly, gasping, almost sobbing with the sweet fulfillment of their desire.

Jennifer moaned as she plummeted through the agonizing, wonderful depths of physical satisfaction. Her body went limp, almost unconscious.

And they lay together for what seemed a long time. Neither was willing to leave the bed. There they were in utter accord. If only the rest of life would be so simple...

When finally they pulled themselves together, took turns in the bathroom and dressed, there was a touchy, uncomfortable feeling between them. Each was overly solicitous of the other, and neither wanted to speak of the events of the night before.

"Well," she said as she poured coffee. "Tonight is your big night."

"Yes." He accepted the mug she offered him and sipped. "Tonight is the night."

"I bought some gag gifts," she said. "Would you mind if we present them after the showing?"

"No, no. That sounds like a good idea. Did you get something for everyone?"

"Well, not everyone," she admitted. "But several."

"Good." He nodded and set down his coffee. "Well. I guess I'd better get moving. Things to do. Places to go. People to meet."

"Yes." She watched him as he strode toward the door. "David?"

He turned back toward her. She had always loved the way he lifted one eyebrow in questioning surprise, but now was not the right time for the serious discussion they must have. "Good luck," she said. "I'll see you tonight."

"Tonight."

Jennifer thoughtfully sipped her coffee, set down the half-finished mug and took off for the store. She needed to be doing something with her hands. Sitting around and worrying was too uncomfortable.

As she kept herself busy through a day that seemed to stretch on forever, she felt a certain bitter anxiety seeping into her conscious. She could call back her ultimatum. The problem was that she'd said exactly what she meant. Sure, she could take care of herself. She didn't need a man around twenty-four hours a day. But she wanted to share with David, to know he would be there for more than fifteen minutes at a time. She desperately wanted to be able to plan for their future.

By late afternoon she settled down behind the counter and began sorting through old photos from the gang at The Lodge. She concentrated on the pictures, trying to figure out which of the more youthful, costumed persons were the people she knew.

She came across a picture that could only be Harriet Kelton and Charlie Peyton, and studied it. It was one of Harriet's later films. Which one? On the back there was a note: *A Quiet Little Murder*, 1949. Jennifer vaguely remembered the plot. Harriet was a whispery-voiced murderer. Whispering?

Jennifer thought of the weird telephone calls. And the whispering voice. Harriet Kelton? That was preposterous! It didn't make any sense, and she certainly couldn't imagine Harriet creeping around the editing studio, leaving tapes in the bushes.

The front doorbell jingled, and Jennifer looked up to see Beth. Her friend looked tired and nervous, and Jennifer remembered in a rush the events of the day before. What had happened between Beth and her husband?

"Beth? How are you feeling? Is everything all right?"

"Sure. Kind of. Philo told me what he was doing late at night, every night." She straightened a stack of discount coupons on the counter and set them down. "It's not another woman. At least, not in the way I thought."

"I'm glad, Beth. But you still seem unhappy. What's old Philo doing, anyway? Tunneling into Continental National Bank?"

"I really shouldn't talk about it."

"Okay." Jennifer reached out to pat her friend's arm. She didn't want to pry. "If you want to talk, I'm here for you, Beth. You know that, don't you?"

Without meeting her gaze Beth nodded.

"Here," Jennifer said, holding up the photo. "Guess who these people are and name this film."

Beth glanced at the photo. "Harriet and Charlie."

"Harriet played a bizarre murderess who never spoke above a whisper. For about two seconds when I first looked at this picture, I cleverly deduced that Harriet was my weird, whispery caller. Crazy, huh? Can you imagine dignified Harriet doing something like that?"

"I have to go, Jennifer."

"Are you sure everything is all right?" Jennifer was worried about Beth. She'd never seen her so nervous.

"Sure. I'll see you tonight."

The evening clerk came in shortly after Beth left, and Jennifer was still standing at the counter, puzzling. What on earth was wrong with Beth?

She went home to change for the grand premiere at Delilah's house. Tonight she meant to take Beth off in a corner and find out what was bothering her. Her friend wasn't the fidgety type. Whatever Philo was doing had truly affected Beth.

Men, Jennifer thought as she slipped into a satiny, clingy Jean Harlow-type dress. When would they understand how much their actions affected their women?

She pulled on the matching jacket, adjusted the padded shoulders and studied herself in the full-length bedroom mirror. Not bad, she decided. The ivory dress played up her light tan and emphasized her slim thighs.

The doorbell rang, and she went to answer. It was Beth.

"You look wonderful," Jennifer greeted her. The blue-and-turquoise swirls in Beth's dress compelled the eye to motion. And Beth's mood—in contrast with earlier in the day—was vivacious.

"We don't have time for chitchat." Beth dashed into the house. "I promised Philo I wouldn't tell you, and he's the partner I'm going to go through life with. But you're my partner, too, Jen. There's no reason you can't guess what he's been up to. Start by thinking about the photograph you showed me."

"Harriet and Charlie," Jennifer said.

"And the part Harriet played in that movie."

"A murderess?" Jennifer looked at Beth as though she were going crazy. "Philo and Harriet are planning a murder?"

"What about the murderess?" Beth urged.

"Well, she whispered all the time." Jennifer gasped. "You mean, I was right? Harriet made those calls? Why?"

"Guess, Jennifer. What did the whisperer keep saying?"

"To leave the past in peace? To think about the future?"

Jennifer remembered Harriet doing those interviews. She kept dragging the topic back to herself and her acting talent and her films. Harriet was still living. She had a future. Clayton Forbes was dead. He was the past.

"Think about Philo and Harriet," Beth urged.

"Well, they hit it off really well. And I know Philo was shooting extra footage of Harriet because David kept complaining about the unnecessary cost." With a thunk all the pieces fell into place. "Philo and Harriet were working late together because they were making their own film. All about Harriet."

"There's more," Beth said. "And this is the worst yet. Think about inventive Charlie Peyton and what happened to you last night."

Jennifer remembered the tape recorder and the whispery voice that caused her to drag David out of the studio. "But nothing happened," she said. "When we came back into the room, everything was exactly the same."

"Did you rerun the Wasp Man film?"

"Oh my God, Beth. Charlie substituted the film Harriet and Philo were working on for the Wasp Man film."

"But I might suggest that you hustle over to the premiere and tell David before he shows those Hollywood executives the wrong film."

Jennifer hugged her friend. "Thanks, Beth."

"Don't thank me. I didn't tell you anything."

Jennifer dashed out the door and hopped into her van. There wasn't much time before the scheduled showing, but she was sure David could find one of the other video copies.

On one hand, she couldn't believe it. Harriet Kelton making weird phone calls? Charlie Peyton skulking around the studio last night, playing tricks? She couldn't imagine them being so malicious. On the other hand, it made very good sense. Harriet and Charlie wouldn't think they were betraying David. Jennifer was sure that they thought they were doing the fledgling producer a favor, showing him the ropes.

She parked in the circular driveway in front of Delilah's huge Colonial-style house and hurried inside. She nodded to several of the local artists and people from The Lodge at Conifer. Delilah's maid served canapés.

Jennifer spied David, chatting with two men who were unfamiliar to her. She rushed over to him and took his arm.

"Jennifer, you look wonderful. I have a couple of people I'd like you to meet."

She politely bobbed her head through the introductions, then said, "Will you gentlemen please excuse us? I need to speak with David alone for a moment."

He shrugged a goodbye to his visiting executives as she hauled him off to a corner. "Which film did you bring?" she asked.

"*Wasp Man Speaks*. There isn't any other film."

"There is. Did you bring the cassette we watched last night?"

"What's going on, Jennifer? I don't get it."

"It's too much to explain. David, you have to get a different copy of the film. Just believe me, all right?"

She looked up to see Philo striding across the room toward them. For the first time since Jennifer had known him, he was dressed in a nicely tailored suit. He carried a videocassette.

"I couldn't let them do it." He handed the cassette to David. "I don't want to screw up your chances, man. This is my copy of *Wasp Man Speaks*."

"I have my copy," David said. "Would you two tell me what the hell is going on?"

"The videocassette you have is a different show," Philo explained. "It's *All About Harriet*. I used a lot of clips from the cutting room floor, and we shot some extra footage, plus some of her own private videos of her films."

"What?"

"Listen, David, I didn't charge you anything for my extra time. Not one dime. And Harriet paid for my extra editing time at Vids 'R' Us. What can I say, man? I'm sorry."

David looked as if he might jump out of his Brooks Brothers suit and strangle Philo. Then a calm came over him. "Is it good?" he asked. "The Harriet film, is it good?"

"Bottom line, it's not as good as *Wasp Man Speaks*." Philo grimaced. "You might say that's one of the reasons I'd rather have these big-time executives see that one."

"I don't believe it," Jennifer said. "I don't believe that's what motivated you, Philo."

He looked at her and shrugged.

"You didn't want to screw David," she said. "That's what made you change your mind."

David cleared his throat. "Whatever. Thanks, Philo."

They all turned toward the front door as Harriet Kelton made her grand entrance. Swathed in white fur with emerald jewelry glittering, she looked every inch the star. Heads swiveled to see her. Though there was no fanfare, she compelled the attention of every person in the room.

"Damn," Philo said. "This is going to break her heart."

# 14

AS DAVID STRODE across the foyer to greet Harriet, Jennifer sighed. In the gracious white foyer of Delilah's home the scene was irresistibly romantic. The resplendent older woman offered her hand, and David gallantly brushed his lips above her bejeweled fingers. As glamorous as Harriet was, David was a match for her. His Clark Gable smile and self-assured posture made a perfect foil for her delicate charm.

"He could have been an actor," Jennifer murmured to Philo. "But thank goodness he's not."

The rest of the people in the room broke into spontaneous applause as David offered Harriet his arm and led her down the two steps into the living room.

Under his breath Philo commented, "The emeralds are a bit much, don't you think?"

She looked at him and sighed. "I don't get it, Philo. How did you get yourself mixed up in this?"

"I'm a jerk, what can I say?"

"You can give me a rational explanation."

"At first I thought I was just doing some experimenting. You know, stretching myself artistically. Then I really wanted to please her. Harriet. She's still got something, Jennifer. I don't know what it is, but there's something about her that made me want to see her become a star again."

"And Charlie Peyton?"

"He's in love with her." Philo shrugged. "I didn't know it at the time, but he was the one responsible for the fire, the 'accident' where the *Wasp Man* tapes were lost. That sneaky little SOB figured that David would have to change the focus of the documentary if he didn't have those clips."

"Did you know he was going to set the fire?"

"No. Not until a couple of days ago when he told me about his plans to switch films. I'm sorry, Jennifer. And I didn't even know about the phone calls until then."

"It's okay," she said. "I wasn't frightened."

"No?"

"Well, maybe last night when I thought I was trapped in the screening room with a psycho whisperer, I was a little tense."

"A little?" Philo asked. "From what I heard, you screamed your head off."

"Perfectly normal reaction."

Beth slipped quietly through the crowd. Her eyes were worried and tense as she glanced back and forth between Philo and Jennifer. Philo wrapped his arm around his wife's waist. "I confessed."

Beth hugged him and beamed at Jennifer. "Tonight," she said, "is going to have a happy ending."

"Do you know something I don't?" Jennifer asked.

"Maybe."

"Listen, partner," Jennifer said. "You're going to have to quit with these pithy predictions. A little more explanation, please."

"We've already done one guessing game. And if you think about David, this won't be a surprise."

They watched as David introduced Harriet to the visiting executives. Harriet managed to seem aloof, regal and warm at the same time. Jennifer shook her head in disbelieving admiration. "She's really something, isn't she?"

"Yeah," Philo agreed. "For a couple of minutes there I was a little in love with her myself. In love with the idea of who she was. I'm going to hate to see her disappointed tonight."

"But you did what was right," Jennifer assured him.

He hugged his wife. "So Beth would tell me. Wouldn't you, honey?"

"You bet I would. Besides, we all know that I am never wrong."

There was a commotion as Delilah wafted through the room and announced, "Let's go, people. Downstairs is the movie room."

Jennifer smiled. Despite her wealth, Delilah was earthy, both feet on the ground. Her major eccentricity was in her eclectic wild artwork. A very large sculpture in one corner showed her fascination with neon. It was a bright blue outline of a man and woman, clasped in embrace. Glowing red hearts interlocked their torsos.

On the way downstairs David joined Jennifer. He linked his arm through hers and gave her a comical leer. "One of our visiting executives has a major crush on you."

She batted her eyelashes. "Obviously the man has taste."

"Your dress is fantastic," he said. "The way the material clings in all the right places. It makes me want to slide it right off your body."

"Something might be arranged," she said.

"I want a definite plan," he returned. "Tonight at your house. Right after we're done here."

"I don't even need to check my appointment book," she said. "I'm free for the evening."

"What about the rest of your life? Put me down for a long-term engagement."

She gazed up at him, slightly confused. "What are you asking, David?"

"Think about it." He found her a third-row seat in Delilah's screening room. "Save the place beside you."

When the assembled group of about twenty people were settled in the large, predominantly orange room, David handed the videocassette to Philo and took a position in front of the screen. "Ladies and gentlemen, welcome to our grand premiere. I want to take this opportunity to thank all of you who helped."

He applauded them, and everyone gleefully joined in backslapping and self-congratulations.

"We have a surprise tonight," David said. "You are all familiar with *Wasp Man Speaks*."

Charlie Peyton sounded the five discordant intro notes, and everyone applauded again.

David focused on Harriet, who was sitting in a place of honor in the front row. "Not many of you are aware that there has been another film under production. A rough cut of *All About Harriet* is ready to be shown. Tonight you will see two films for the price of one."

Delilah piped up, "And since they're both no charge, it's a real deal."

Philo gave an exuberant whoop of pure pleasure before he hit the lights, and *Wasp Man Speaks* began.

Jennifer reveled in the display of her watercolor paintings of Clayton Forbes that showed beneath the opening credits. When David worked his way through the crowd to sit beside her, she grinned and took his hand. She was so pleased with him. Showing both films was the very best thing he could have done. She squeezed his hand.

He leaned close to her ear and spoke softly. "I couldn't deny her this moment of glory."

Jennifer felt tears of pride stinging her eyes. "You did the right thing."

"Compromise," he said. "I learned that when I was a banker. Anything is possible with cooperation and compromise."

Throughout the showing for this very, very appreciative audience, Jennifer felt incredibly close to David. He'd done well in producing the documentary. His career was launched.

"It's terrific," she said softly.

"You, Jennifer Watt, are terrific."

He covered her hand with both of his. Her fingers were so slender and delicate. It was hard for him to realize there was so much artistic skill in that little hand.

Like the old-fashioned guy he was, David caressed her hand with a "put her up on a pedestal" reverence. These fingers should never have to work hard. This hand should be... He stopped himself. This was Jennifer. If she wasn't the way she was, he would not love her so well.

Throughout the premiere he kept stealing peeks at her profile. She looked so fine and pale in the darkness. He couldn't wait until after the grand premiere. Then he would turn their relationship into something committed and permanent. They would never be apart again.

He stood to acknowledge the applause from the audience at the finale of the Wasp Man documentary. Then Philo started the second feature.

With a critical eye David studied the Harriet Kelton film. It wasn't as well orchestrated as the Clayton Forbes biography, but it showed promise, and Philo's cinematography was exceptionally good. Some of the cuts were a bit sloppy, he noted. And the voice-over was corny. With editing and rewriting he thought it would make a fine second film for the PBS series.

What would he have done if Philo and Harriet had presented him with the idea? He probably would have refused. His decision, however, would have been based in part on the overbudget Wasp Man production. If he'd known he could get two films at this price, he might have okayed the extra videotape. But maybe not.

He'd needed a tribute to Uncle Clayton Forbes. David had needed to immerse himself in the lore of the man who had secretly influenced his life. With *Wasp Man Speaks* completed, David felt a joyful separation from his uncle. That was Forbes—on the film. His uncle had accomplished much in his life. But David's life was separate. He was free from the past and a wonderful future lay before him. A life with Jennifer, he thought.

When the lights went on, he and Jennifer made their way through the milling, happy throng to the executives. David knew their reaction would be a verdict. If they hated the films, he could kiss some of his distribution revenue goodbye.

All four men were smiling. "It's good," one of them said.

"The Kelton one needs work," another put in.

"But it's only a rough cut."

"I never knew that Forbes did all that stuff. Or Kelton."

"The career changes are amazing."

"Hard to realize that someone could be in silents, talkies and television."

"Gentlemen," David said. "Do we have a deal?"

Three heads nodded. Three of the men shook hands with David. They turned to the fourth man. "What do you think, Lester?"

"It depends," he said.

"Depends on what?" David asked.

The man from Hollywood looked directly at Jennifer. "Does she have a sister?"

"I do," Jennifer said. "And she lives in Ohio with her husband and three kids."

"Well, Davey, boy," Lester relented. "I guess I liked the films, anyway. You got a deal."

Upstairs, where Delilah's maid had replenished the buffet and opened more wine bottles, they mingled. Jennifer broke away from David for a moment and recruited Charlie Peyton to help her bring in the gag gifts from the van.

As they stood at the entrance, she turned to him. "You know, Charlie, you don't need schemes and plans."

He gave her a wide-eyed, innocent look.

"Most of your ideas are good. If you tell people directly what you want, you might be surprised."

"How so?"

"You might just get what you're after." She patted his arm. "And if you ever pull anything like that sneaky routine at the studio when you switched the tapes, I'll rip your face off."

"Food for thought," he said, following her inside.

Jennifer called for silence, but it wasn't until Delilah sounded her two-fingered whistle that the room stilled. Jennifer took a position at the steps leading from the foyer. She raised her voice. "Everybody who worked on and around this film deserves an Academy Award."

There was loud cheering.

"I have modest substitutes," she offered. "For Beth, the scriptwriter, a four-foot-tall pencil."

Charlie held up the prize. As Beth came forward to accept her gift, Jennifer added, "With an appropriately large eraser."

She presented Philo with a gilded flashbulb.

Wanda, the film editor, got a pair of gilded scissors.

For Delilah, their hostess, Jennifer had found a sculpture of a bronco, very similar to the one that reared at Mile High Stadium.

For several of the actors from The Lodge she produced small silver stars with their names engraved across them.

From her purse she pulled out Charlie Peyton's present—a shiny trumpet. "Only to be used for announcing Wasp Man."

"For Harriet Kelton," Jennifer said. "I wish this was an Oscar." She held up a very large silver star.

"And for David Constable, the man who made everything possible." Jennifer turned to Charlie, who set up David's gift—a director's chair with his name stenciled across the back. "Come here and try it out," she said.

Everyone applauded as David made a great show of arranging his bottom in the chair. He rose and signaled for quiet. "This is ironic," he said. "Because I've also found the perfect present for Jennifer."

Delilah came forward. She was carrying a director's chair.

Jennifer laughed. "We got each other the same thing?"

"Not exactly," he said.

He swiveled the chair around to reveal the name stenciled on the back: Jennifer Watt-Constable.

There was considerable ooohing and aaahing from the group assembled. For once Jennifer didn't know what to do. She was taken completely by surprise. "David," she stammered. "I...I don't know what to say."

The crowd of artists and actors responded for her. "Say yes," they shouted.

"I'll do better than that."

There couldn't have been a more public place, and that prim little being who lived within Jennifer was appalled as she slid her arms up David's chest and around his neck. She pulled him close. "Here's looking at you, kid," she said softly.

Amid encouraging cheers, she kissed him like there was no tomorrow. Her tongue slipped lightly between his lips, teasing and accepting. And she felt him responding, holding her tightly.

As if their actions were choreographed, they took their seats in the director's chairs, holding hands and smiling.

"And now," Delilah announced. "A toast."

They held their glasses aloft as Delilah pronounced, "To the marvelous quest we all follow. May David and Jennifer have found a part of their dreams."

"To the quest."

Delilah's example started a series of toasts from practically everybody.

It was after midnight when David and Jennifer finally broke away and drove to her house. At the doorway David paused. "May I carry you over the threshold?"

"Why not?"

He swooped her inside. "Now that we're alone, I want to make certain. Jennifer, will you marry me?"

"I thought you'd never ask."

They sealed their vows with another kiss, even more intimate than the first. Jennifer vaguely wondered if she would ever tire of kissing David. Never, she answered herself, not as long as these wonderful feelings came when their lips met.

"About that promotional tour," he said.

Her heart sank, and she moved away from him. "Oh, David. Don't go. I want to be married tomorrow. I want to start having a real relationship."

"I have a compromise," he offered. "I know it's not much of a honeymoon, but how would you feel about an expenses-paid trip to Kansas City, Milwaukee, Chicago, Wichita—"

"Honeymoon?"

"It makes it a lot easier to register in hotels."

"You have trouble with that, don't you? Registering in hotels."

"Only when I want the lady I'm escorting to be my wife."

She considered for a moment. Their relationship, she thought with satisfaction. The time for silent worry was at an end. Their relationship was a reality with form and substance. It existed. Their love would provide the nurturing and compromise would provide the solutions.

She'd changed so much from the first time they'd met. Under the neon lights during that summer rainstorm, she couldn't have imagined leaving her shop for a month. Now he had a stable business partner in Beth. And there was something more in her life than responsibility and duty. There was David.

She stepped into his waiting embrace.

"You know that I'll come with you," she said. "Now what's your half of the compromise?"

"One week in Malibu every month?"

"This is beginning to sound a little one-sided."

"If it doesn't work out, I promise to quit the monthly trip."

*Sand between my toes*, she thought. It might not be so torturous to adjust to a monthly beach jaunt. And she could set up a permanent art studio in the office area with the skylights.

Jennifer grinned up at him. "It's the craziest thing, but as soon as you said you'd give it up, I wanted to give it a try."

"That's not crazy. It's you."

"So, David. Where do we go after Wichita?"

"I can't remember," he said, lifting her off her feet. "But I know where I'd like to go right now."

"One more promise?"

"Name it." He nuzzled her throat.

"If we ever buy a house together," she said, "we have to have one of those long flights of stairs, like in *Gone With the Wind*. Then we can play Rhett and Scarlett every day."

"Frankly, my dear—" he carried her into the bedroom "—I *do* give a damn."

# Harlequin Temptation

# COMING NEXT MONTH

### #173 HEAT WAVE Barbara Delinsky
She couldn't handle the heat, and neither could her neighbor. Night after night, barely clothed and seeking a cool breeze, Caroline Cooper and Brendan Carr eyed each other across the courtyard. And ached for the moment when they would finally meet....

### #174 HERO IN DISGUISE Gina Wilkins
Even though Summer Reed didn't realize it yet, Derek Anderson knew he was the hero to satisfy all her requirements—and then some. But he would take his time. Although he crashed her party, from then on his assault on her senses was devastatingly subtle....

### #175 WHERE MEMORIES BEGIN Elizabeth Glenn
As a teenager, Lanni Preston had fallen for a gorgeous but mysterious youth, Chandler Scott. When he suddenly returned ten years later, Lanni was fully grown, and her womanly responses to him were more powerful than a girl's tender longing. But the man was still mysterious....

### #176 A WANTED MAN Regan Forest
Kirk Hawthorne was one cowboy that brand inspector Beth Connor intended to stick to like a burr. He might not be a horse thief, but he dared to steal her heart, committing the ultimate crime of passion....

**An intriguing story
of a love that defies the boundaries of time.**

## BEVERLY SOMMERS

## Time and Again

Knocked unconscious by a violent earthquake, Lauren, a computer operator, wakes up to find that she is no longer in her familiar world of the 1980s, but back in 1906. She not only falls into another era but also into love, a love she had only known in her dreams. Funny...heartbreaking...always entertaining.

Available in August or reserve your copy for July shipping by sending your name, address, zip or postal code along with a check or money order for $4.70 (includes 75¢ for postage and handling) payable to Worldwide Library to:

| In the U.S. | In Canada |
| --- | --- |
| Worldwide Library | Worldwide Library |
| 901 Fuhrmann Blvd. | P.O. Box 609 |
| Box 1325 | Fort Erie, Ontario |
| Buffalo, NY 14269-1325 | L2A 5X3 |

Please specify book title with your order.

**WORLDWIDE LIBRARY**

TIM-1

# What readers say about Harlequin Temptation...

One word is needed to describe the series Harlequin Temptation... "Exquisite." They are so sensual, passionate and beautifully written.
—H.D., Easton, PA

I'm always looking forward to the next month's Harlequin Temptation with a great deal of anticipation...
—M.B., Amarillo, TX

I'm so glad you now have Harlequin Temptation... the stories seem so real. They really stimulate my imagination!
—S.E.B., El Paso, TX

Names available on request.